VIVI CONWAY

Published by Knights Of
Knights Of Ltd, Registered Offices:
119 Marylebone Road, London, NW1 5PU

www.knightsof.media
First published 2023
001

Written by Lizzie Huxley-Jones
Text and cover copyright © Lizzie Huxley-Jones, 2023
Cover art by © Harry Woodgate, 2023
All rights reserved
The moral right of the author and illustrator has been asserted

Set in Baskerville
Typeset design by Sophie McDonnell
Typeset by Sophie McDonnell
Printed and bound in the UK

All rights reserved. No part of this publication may be
reproduced or transmitted in any form or by any means,
electronic or mechanical, including photocopying, recording,
or any information storage or retrieval system, without prior
permission in writing from the publishers. If you are
reading this, thank you for buying our book.

A CIP catalogue record for this book will be
available from the British Library

ISBN: 9781913311421

VIVI CONWAY

AND THE
SWORD OF LEGEND

Lizzie Huxley-Jones

KO
KNIGHTS OF

For my parents, Aliy and Keith,
who showed me the stories and
let me run wild in them.

Chapter One

The problem with growing up listening to bedtime stories about monsters, magic and myth is that you don't really question it when a lake summons you.

The lake, my lake, is calling to me, and has been for about a week. It's a pull in my chest, a gnawing in my brain. I couldn't tell you *how* I know it's the lake, but I feel it in my bones when I'm awake, and it's woken me up several times, as though someone has been calling my name.

And the worst part of it all is that it doesn't weird me out. That much.

Maybe my understanding of what is "normal" is a little, erm, warped. But you don't grow up autistic and weird without realising your version of normal is quite different from everyone else's.

1

Mumma's stories definitely haven't helped there either.

A sensible person might question why a whole load of water would be almost-talking to them, never mind how that could even happen. And I get it, it's weird. But, somehow, I know I have to be there. To listen, maybe? To find . . . something. I don't know. Nothing is clear.

I just know that I have to go and say goodbye to the lake. Like the way you know when it's going to rain, or when a cake will turn out just right. Mumma always calls those feelings "kitchen witchery", but I always thought it was just luck or something like that.

A goodbye is probably all it wants, right?

It all started the day Mam came back from London, having set up the new house ready for us to move into. The Mums had decided we'd move away from Wales at the start of summer. Mumma's work had been trying to promote her to the London office for years, but she didn't want to uproot me when I'd finally got comfortable. Then, things went bad.

Kelly Keane and I had been best friends since we were in nursery and I hadn't needed more friends, because I had Kelly. But then she met Danielle, and then Paul came along too. Neither of them liked me. And soon, neither did Kelly. At first, I kept going to school, but everything quickly went from bad to worse . . .

After I missed the last three months of Year Six, the Mums decided a fresh start would be a good thing for us, and by that point I was so tired I just said yes. I would be starting secondary school along with everyone else in September, but not in Wales. In London. But being the new kid would probably work in my favour. If everyone already had their friend groups from primary school, maybe no one would bother me. I hoped so.

Anyway, that night, the Mums and I sat around our craggy old table eating peanut butter noodles when a huge rainstorm appeared from nowhere, rattling the windows of our old farmhouse. There'd even been flooding throughout the valley, so the farmers had had to go out and rescue their sheep, moving them to safety.

And ever since that storm, ever since I realised we really were leaving, I've heard the call. It's kind of taken over my brain, clouding out any other thought.

I had thought, to start with, that it was just the usual anxiety about things changing. My therapist Dr. May says that most autistic people struggle with change and newness, and we'd spent the summer talking through my worries about moving and having to start going to school again.

But, as I lie here at five in the morning on the day we move house (and country). I can finally, *really* hear it. It's a half-heard whisper. *Come here. Come look.*

I have to go, and that means sneaking out before the Mums wake up.

I've never snuck out before. We live miles from the next village, surrounded by farmland in the gap between towns, the sort of house you pass on the way to somewhere else. Plus, I really can't lie. My face always gives away exactly what I'm thinking, and the Mums can spot a half-truth from across a room. I don't like lies, even the ones that are supposed to be kind to spare people's feelings when the truth isn't very nice. If I insisted I had to go, the Mums probably would take me to the lake. But moving day means a schedule that probably shouldn't be messed with, and they both seem really stressed out – Mumma keeps doing this weird pasted-on smile every time I ask her something, while Mam just spends all the time making lists and aggressively chewing gum. It just makes more sense for me to go while they're asleep.

Slipping out from under the covers, I lightly avoid

the creakiest floorboards around my bed. In an old farmhouse, that's easier said than done. The light outside is a golden dawn, the weather finally clearing. I empty my backpack out onto the bed and cover the things I had packed for the car with the duvet. It isn't a convincing person-in-bed substitute, but it's the best I can do given all my stuff is in boxes. Thanks to Mam's trusty black Sharpie and slightly intense moving organisation system, I find my rash guard and swimming shorts quickly, throwing them into my backpack. If I'm going to go all the way up there, I may as well swim too.

There's no point changing into today's clothes and getting them potentially mucky, so I just pull on my warmest knitted jumper and bright raincoat over my pyjamas. Hopefully no one will spot me in luminous yellow; in Wales you can never be too prepared for rain.

I creep out, and go down the stairs on my bum, just to be safe. All the rugs that usually cover every floor are rolled up in tubes downstairs, so every step echoes around the empty hallways.

Something gets caught in my hair. I leap away, holding my breath so I don't yell, and bat whatever it is away from my face. Squinting through the darkness and hoping I've not just destroyed a spider's hard work – I'd feel bad about ruining their webs, but also would rather not have their packed lunch flies in my bird's nest of hair – I see that luckily it's just the last of Mam's lavender, picked from the hillside and hanging up to dry. I let out the breath, and pad through the empty kitchen.

My muddy yellow wellies wait at the back door ready to be slung in the boot of the car, and I wriggle them on, wincing at the cool damp inside. The big bronze key is in its usual place on the spice shelf, even though that's now totally empty. It turns easily in the lock, and I close the door behind me with one quick, quiet tug.

I find my bike leaning against the side of the house, and walk it down our drive, just in case I immediately crash loudly into something while trying to be stealthy.

Helmet on. Bike light lit. Mysterious expedition to a lake in the wee hours of the morning without any supervision is officially go.

The roads are completely empty, though I can already hear Mr. Bevan, one of the farmers, starting up his tractor somewhere in the distance. It's not quiet in the country, though everyone thinks that. Sheep call to each other as they wake up, and insects buzz. Birds sing from the hedgerows that border the winding roads. A bat flits through the air ahead of me, catching the last night-time bugs before it goes to roost. I want to slow down, to watch the nature I grew up with wake up for one last time, but I can't get caught out here. Everyone knows everyone around here, and I'm the only kid who ever goes up to the lake, so anyone awake at this time would know that it's me, that weird scruffy Conway girl. No one else from school goes up there unless they're dragged by their parents; they all say I'm some kind of pond-loving weirdo.

It probably is a bad idea, but once I'm away from the house, pedalling hard, I stop caring. I just want to be in the lake one last time. My lake, which is actually called Llyn (Arian), is bright blue ice-cold crystal water and sits at the foot of a group of mountains. I've been swimming there at least once a week since I was small, when Mumma got really into outdoor swimming. One year she made us go on Boxing Day when snow had runoff from the peaks, but that was kind of torturous and luckily never repeated.

Soon I'm off the road and onto the walker's path, which leads up to the lake. I breathe a sigh of relief that I've passed no one, or at least I'm pretty sure

I haven't. Years of cycling here means I make quick work of it – I know where all the potholes are, where it gets muddiest, where rabbits like to dash across.

But also, the pull in my brain seems to be getting louder, turning into a buzz. And the closer I get, the more frantic it sounds. The pulling-buzzing-drumming makes my legs churn faster.

Over the rise, glistening in the morning light, is my lake. Turquoise and gold-light dappled, the clearest water I've ever seen. In the low light, it looks lorded over by the peaks of mountains on three sides. People around here say it was a seat of power for giants, maybe even their throne. The air is so fresh.

An ache blooms in my chest. This is the last time I'll be here for . . . I can't even imagine how long.

I don't know how to be a London person. In Wales, I can follow the seasons with the changing colours, and when the wind blows the right way I can taste salt from the sea, sharp and sour on my tongue. And I know the land, because of Mumma's stories. When I was small, Mumma used to take me out walking, just the two of us. The night before, she would tell me a story set in the place we were going to visit, and the next day we would look for proof of the myths. I was so determined that one day I'd find a door in a tree trunk, a keyhole in a stone, even a hidden castle. I always hoped I'd find a whole other world, that I'd discover magic. That I'd be part of something bigger than just this.

But now I'm leaving, so I guess that hope has to stay here. I'll leave it in the water.

I lay my bike on the grass, throwing off my rucksack with it. No one is around, so I drop my pyjamas in a crumpled heap and slip into my swimming kit.

Get in the water. Go on.

It must be my own thoughts, but . . . it doesn't sound like me. I shake it off and stand at the water's edge in the muddy sand.

Some people like to test the temperature with a toe before they get in, but I think the best way is to just stride in purposefully. So, I do, breathing deeply in shock as the icy water laps against my belly. The water is chilled by the night.

A little way out, I float on my back, and every muscle relaxes. The water threads through my mussed-up hair.

And finally, the pulling starts to dull, like a released breath. Relieved that my brain feels finally clear, I dive down below the surface, kicking hard with my legs.

My tummy skims along the lake bed. I love seeing how far I can go on a single breath.

Just as I'm about to surface for air, I see a moving shadow in the distance. A quick dart, like a fish. A *big* fish. I didn't know there were any in here.

I break the surface and wipe away the hair matted on my face. What was that?

I tread water, watching for any movement. A fluttering feeling grows in my stomach as I realise everything is really, really quiet. The gnawing in my head is gone. And so are all the sounds of the country. No birdsong, no insects, no sheep.

Across the lake, the water starts to stir. It's . . . a wave? Waves don't just appear in lakes.

My heart pounds in my chest. Maybe coming here was a mistake. I should get out, quickly.

Before I can finish the thought, the wave grows, white-tipped, a tsunami ready to drown me.

And inside the wave, I can see the shadow. It is much, much bigger than I thought. Whatever is in the water with me is definitely not a fish. Its shape is all wrong.

There's a monster in the lake, and it's coming right towards me.

Chapter Two

I swim as fast as I can towards the nearest bank.

No one knows I'm here.

It's just me, and a monster.

I pump my arms furiously, trying to keep the rhythm of my front crawl. I was never the fastest in swimming races. Mam says I'm built for stamina, not speed. Not ideal when you're trying to escape something chasing you.

How naive I had been to hope for keyholes and portals and secret castles. Maybe a magical school, or a friendly talking animal. Of course I'd end up with a monster that seems keen on drowning me. I take back every silly hope for magic. I take it all back.

I turn my head to breathe, and a heavy wave lands on top of me. I crash down through the water, slamming hard against the lake bed. My body is battered by the current, pushing me down into the muck one moment, then dragging me slowly backwards the next; towards whatever is headed towards me. I scramble in the dirt, trying to right myself, but the current twists me round.

Stay calm, Vivi. I press my lips together – if I breathe in a big gulp of lake water, it's all over.

With one big push I'm upright and kicking off the floor, eyes on the shimmering surface. It's so close. My lungs burn, my pulse thundering in my ears. I need air fast.

My fingers break through to the air, just as something grabs my ankle and pulls me down sharply. Back on the muddy lake bed, I look back to see a churning rope-current of water wrapped around my leg.

It can't be real. Water doesn't move like it's *alive.*

The rope drags me by the leg, back towards the deep dark cold of the lake. It's sharp, digging into my skin with an icy-cold pain.

Dark spots appear in my vision, and I know there's hardly any time left before my body is going to try to breathe or I pass out.

My fingers rake through the thick black mud,

grabbing onto weak knotted weeds and smooth glass bottles that give way. I can barely see anything from the dirt and the waves and how quickly I'm being dragged, but suddenly there's a tall glint of grey and I grab it tightly.

And somehow it holds.

The rope tugs insistently at my leg, but I don't move.

The silt settles in the water, and I realise what I'm clutching isn't a pillar of rock. It's a sword, stabbed right into the lake-muck. I don't have time to wonder why there's a sword in here. My arm muscles scream as I hold on against the insistent yanking on my leg.

One problem solved – I'm no longer moving. But I'm still definitely about to run out of air. I can taste iron, where I've bitten too hard on the inside of my mouth to keep it closed and drawn blood. I've got one chance to escape.

The sword. Use the sword.

The words ring in my ears. A whispering voice through the pounding of my own heart.

It's my only option, and I don't have time to wonder who might be talking to me. Mysterious messages were how I got in this mess in the first place.

I rip the sword out of the mud, and, sensing the

lack of resistance, the rope yanks me back.

With the last bit of my strength, I swipe the blade through the rushing current at the water-rope around my ankle. To my surprise, it cuts through and the rope vanishes.

I'm free.

I tuck the sword, hilt first, into the back of my swimming shorts and swim hard, breaking the surface in seconds. The sweet air is delicious but stings my sore lungs.

Unfortunately, I really am in the centre of the lake. I have a long way to swim.

The water thrums, and I swim as fast as I can, frantic energy coursing through my body. I've made something very, very angry, but I'm not sticking around to find out what it is.

The thrums become waves quickly, knocking my body back and forth. I fight hard to swim through the roiling water, diving under the waves whenever I can.

Keep going! Keep going!

I sure will, I think, relieved that the voice seems invested in me staying alive. I keep powering forward, and soon my foot touches something solid.

Scrabbling to my feet, I run – but there's more resistance than feels normal. The water slips past me, like sand in an hourglass.

Don't look back.

I cry out in relief as my feet hit grass, and I limp towards my things.

But then, because I am quite possibly a complete donkey, I look backwards. Where I was just swimming is damp sand, covered in sagging plants and fish drowning in the air. What remains of the lake is now a swirling whirlpool.

And, right in the middle of it is a long reptilian snout.

Unfortunately, I know exactly what it is.

An afanc. Flooder of towns and murderer of maidens. Or at least, that's what all Mumma's stories said. Think of the most terrifying, gigantic alligator you can, and you'd be halfway there. Dark green scales that shine in the dawn light, and a long muscular tail, flat and wide like a beaver's, which spins the water faster and faster. It looks right at me and I swear it smiles, baring a snarl of barbed-wire teeth.

It's the most horrible thing I've ever seen, and unfortunately it seems like it really, really wants to kill me.

Our eyes are locked on each other, and time slows down as I rewind Mumma's stories in my memory.

How did they defeat it? There was one where some huge oxen dragged it up a mountain to a lake . . . after singing it to sleep. That's not going to work. My voice is more like the wails of a cat being given a bath, rather than the melody of a beautiful maiden.

It opens its mouth wider and roars a horrible nail-on-chalkboard sound that echoes around the peaks. There's absolutely no cover between me and the afanc. It has a straight shot right towards me, and I don't think there's any way I can outrun it, though I keep walking backwards slowly and steadily.

Wait! Peredur, the Knight of King Arthur, slew an afanc by cutting off its head while he held an adder stone that turned him invisible. I might not have invisibility, but I do have a sword.

Freeing it from my shorts, I clutch it so hard in my hands that my knuckles turn white. Somehow, the grip fits perfectly in my small shaking hands. It's short, stubby, and green with algae.

The sword hums in my hand, and I realise it's the very same sound that has been rattling around in my head for two weeks. But now it's softer, like it's saying *hello* rather than gnawing at me. Is this what drew me here?

As if it heard me thinking about stabbing it, the afanc opens its maw and shoots out more water tentacles, throwing them like spears. I dodge, jump, and scrabble as several whip past my head. As I scramble to my feet, realising I've leapt right back into the slippery, damp sand of the lake bed, a long tentacle of water whips me hard in the chest. I fly through the air and land hard in oozing black muck. The sword skids out of reach, landing in the grass.

If I thought not being able to breathe underwater was bad, I'm now completely winded. My sides screech as I gasp. I can't get enough air, which is an unfortunate running theme today.

All foolish notions of beheading the afanc leave me as I cough, spitting up a gob of bloody goo. Plan B – getting out of here preferably without dying – is back on. I stagger to my feet, wincing in agony, but as I step towards the sword I fall to my knees.

Keep going!

I can't stand, so I grit my teeth and drag myself on all fours, feeling like I'm climbing a mountain rather than scuttling through muck. My limbs shake with effort, and more water spears slide across my path, missing me by centimetres.

It's mocking me. It knows I can't stop it.

The afanc bellows, and the sound feels like eighteen people are speaking all at once. The sound is so wrong that I'm dizzy with it. It echoes through my head, battering against my skull. My brain aches with it, and I can barely stay conscious.

This is it. I'm alone, and I'm going to die here.

Moving, and all the change, doesn't feel quite so scary anymore.

I close my eyes and think of the Mums. *I'm sorry. I'm sorry for this, for everything.*

Salty tears and snot and blood mix on my lips.

"Get up! Come on, get up!"

Someone is shouting at me. Actually shouting at me, not a disembodied voice in my mind.

I'm not alone.

I open my mouth to reply, but a hacking cough rattles my body and up comes more water. Before I can move, another water tentacle glides across the surface of the water and winds up my leg like creeping bramble. It tightens, digging into my skin. Crushing my leg.

Angry heat burns through my chest, as I screech in pain.

I refuse to die at the hands, or claws, of what is

basically a giant beaver.

Fury floods my body, and I scream.

"GET OFF ME!"

And, to my surprise, it actually does. The tentacle collapses into water droplets, seeping into the ground. To my even greater surprise, so does the whirlpool. Half of it spills back into being a lake, and the afanc screeches with fury as its tail tries to whip it back into shape. It screeches again, a sound I feel in my blood, and I swoon like I'm going to faint.

"Woah, that was neat!"

Suddenly, the person who shouted at me is by my side, helping me stand. They must be about my age, but where I'm small and chubby, they are broad and tall. Thick auburn hair flops near their bright sea-green eyes.

"Hiya, I'm Dara," they say. "And this is Gelert."

At that, a huge grey dog appears next to me. It's still within the realm of dog sizes, unlike the enormous afanc across the water, but it's far bigger than any of the farmers' sheepdogs.

"Gel, get them to safety. And nobody touch the water!" Dara barks, running full pelt towards the afanc.

The dog takes my rash guard in its mouth and drags me up the beach towards the sand. It's so strong and I'm so weak that I just stagger after it.

"No, stop!" I try to scream, but I'm so weak that nothing comes out.

I'm barely awake, on the edge of passing out. My feet touch grass, and I collapse onto my bum as the dog stops dragging me, satisfied that we're far enough away.

In the distance, I see a tiny Dara rush to the edge of the water that fell out of the whirlpool.

And, with a great yell that echoes against the mountain peaks, they plunge their hands deep into the lake and everything around us lights up.

The air turns royal purple, and the afanc shakes violently as the light touches it.

No, not light.

Electricity.

With one last bone-rattling cry, it falls. Defeated, it sinks into the deep.

In a blink of an eye, as though nothing happened, the lake is as it's always been. The water reaches the shore again, no longer tied up in a whirlpool. It shines azure blue in the brighter morning light.

And with that, everything goes black.

Chapter Three

I hear birdsong.

My eyes flicker open, but everything is still blurry from the muck and water.

"Oh Gelert, they're awake," I hear my saviour, Dara, say.

I rub my eyes clear with the back of my hand, hoping that it is less dirty than my disgustingly muddy fingers. Slowly, everything begins to sharpen. I'm still at the lake, and the lake looks normal again.

"Here, drink this." Dara holds out a can of lemonade. Beads of condensation glisten on the metal. I never want fizzy drinks before lunch, never mind breakfast, but after almost drowning it's exactly what I need.

I ease myself up to sitting, wincing with the ache

in my chest, and take the freshly opened can. The sickly-sweet sugar floods through my battered body.

"Thanks for this," I pant. "And for saving me."

"All in a day's work," they say, a smile reaching their sparkling eyes. Their cheeks and nose are pink with the cool morning air.

A sharp pain rushes through my head, and everything starts to come back to me. An afanc. And purple light? The sword. Did it all really happen? I press my hands firmly against my temples and, after a moment, the pain begins to ease.

Dara pulls a blanket out of their backpack and wraps it around my shoulders. The rough wool is warm against my cold, clammy skin.

"Rescuing people from monsters at the crack of dawn, sounds like a weird job," I say, before taking another long slow gulp of lemonade.

"Well, someone's got to do it." It comes out flat, like a tired truth, but I figure they are joking along with me, and that I'm too tired to get it, so I smile back.

"I'm Vivi by the way," I say.

"Hi Vivi," they say. "Are you alright? Not hurt I hope?"

"My ribs," I say, with a wheeze. My sides are tight,

and ache with each breath. After a beat, I add, "Are you?"

"Nah, I'm fine. I think you'd annoyed it enough that it wasn't paying enough attention to me."

"It was an afanc, wasn't it?"

"Yup."

"Why?"

"Why was it an afanc?"

"Why was it here? I don't understand what just happened to me . . ."

They run their fingers through their damp hair. "It's a long story."

There's something about the way they say it that makes me think I don't want to hear it. Perhaps if I just get up and leave, I can pretend this never happened.

Go home. Wait, home. *Moving.* Oh no, how long have I been here?

"What time is it?" I ask.

They glance down at the shiny chrome watch on their wrist. "Almost seven."

"Urgh, I've got to get home," I moan. I try to stand, but my legs tremble with the effort.

"No, please," they say, reaching towards me with

arms outstretched. "Sit down. Rest. We'll help you get home once you've got your strength."

I give in. There is no way I can get home on my own right now. "Okay," I concede.

"Do you live far from here?"

"My house is the big blue one in the valley. Mam decided it should stand out so we can always find our way home."

"That's cute."

"It is," I say, with a pang in my chest. I won't be looking for a blue house any more. "Do you live around here?"

They shake their head. "No. Just visiting."

Visiting where, I think. And why? This bit of Wales isn't easy to get to in the daytime, never mind before most of the country is awake.

My head throbs again.

"Wait, what do you mean *we*? And wasn't there a dog here?"

And in front of me, as though I had summoned it, appears a dog. Like, right out of thin air.

"I'm dreaming. I must be dreaming," I mutter, pinching at the skin on my hand sharply. But I'm not dreaming.

"Gelert," chides Dara. "You're not supposed to do that in front of new people. Look, you've freaked her out."

The dog seems to shrug his great shoulders, then yawns in a way that shows off his huge white teeth and bright pink tongue.

One year when we had the flu, Mam and I watched all of Crufts and since then, I've remembered all the dog breeds. This dog is an enormous shaggy Irish Wolfhound, with long legs and huge doe eyes nestled in silver-grey fur.

What Crufts didn't prepare me for, was the possibility that it might talk.

"Eh, let off, will you?" he moans to Dara, before turning back to me. "What? You want me to introduce myself or something? Alright, I'm Gelert."

A talking dog.

An afanc.

Someone with magical light powers.

This is real, somehow. Things from Mumma's stories, but actually happening to me.

Like the stories were true all along.

I'm torn. The bit of me that loves the stories buzzes with excitement; the part that was longing for a new, quieter, life is getting ready to run.

Normally I'd hold out a hand for a dog to sniff, so they can decide in their own time if they want to come closer. But this dog just spoke to me. How are you supposed to greet a talking dog?

I can't believe I ever wanted a talking animal companion. The reality is just . . . too weird.

"But . . . *who* are you? Why are you here? What is going on?"

"Gelert. I did say it, didn't I mun?"

The dog's accent is Welsh, but I can't place where he could be from. It's thick, all rolled Rs and dropped Hs.

"Do you think she hit her head? Maybe she's coming over all silly, like. ARE YOU ALRIGHT GIRL?" He shouts very slowly.

I start to cry. I didn't even know there were talking dogs, and now there's one yelling at me.

"Argh Gelert, you're so rude," Dara hisses, passing me a pack of tissues from their bag. I take one and blow my nose loudly.

The dog sits, and haughtily turns his snout away from us. "Well now, I didn't think she'd bat an eye at me chatting after the calonnau and all this mess up here." Here comes out like 'yurr'.

"I hadn't gotten to that yet! You're mucking it all up," they whine, narrowing their eyes. "I told you not to leave."

"Someone had to check old croc-face was dead."

"And is it?"

"Disappeared." Gelert sniffs.

"So does that mean it is or it isn't dead?"

They bicker for a little longer, and I'm so tired I don't even hear what they're saying. That happens a lot to me; if there are multiple sounds at once, or if I'm feeling too tired, my brain just doesn't process it. They stop for long enough that my brain manages to catch up, so I hear when Dara says, "Sorry, I probably should have led with *the dog talks and is a grumpy guts.*"

"I'll give you grumpy guts," mutters the dog, who disappears. A few blinks later, he returns. In his mouth is the sword from the lake.

He lays it down at my feet. The blade is silver, beneath all the algae and lake grime. The grip is decorated in vines and flowers, and, as I pick off the muck with a fingernail, I find an engraving of a dragon at the bottom.

"I wonder whose sword this is," I murmur.

"I know the answer," says the dog smugly.

"Gelert," warns Dara.

"I'll be gentle," he says. "Who owns it is a bit complicated as it stands. But I can tell you it's called Excalibur."

"Excalibur?" I gasp, turning the sword over. It hums in my hands as I inspect it. "Excalibur as in King Arthur's sword?"

"Aye, that's the one."

"How do I have King Arthur's sword? Why was it here?" I whisper.

"Do you know much about Excalibur?" asks Dara gently.

"Bits. I've seen the Disney version of *The Sword in the Stone*, and Mumma's told me a few local stories, but she says there's different versions of Arthur in different countries."

The dog stands and begins to slowly pace back and forth in front of me. "Well, the first bit to know is that Excalibur isn't the sword that was stuck in that blinking great rock, so you can forget about that. That sword got lost in a dual against King Pellinore, very early on, like. And so, because he didn't have a sword any more, Arthur went to speak to the Gwraig Annwn."

"Wait, do you mean water fairies?" I ask, remembering the illustrations in Mumma's books.

He pauses, watching me. A tufted eyebrow slowly raises. "I was getting to that," he huffs.

"Sorry," I mutter.

"They are not 'water fairies'," he huffs. "Gwraig Annwn are aquatic, look a bit like you humans, and can pass between our world and the world of Other."

"I always thought they were like mermaids," I say, trying to remember which stories involved them, but my head just spins.

"No, that's a morgen," he sniffs. "You know when you've got a morgen because they reek."

Something catches my eye. Through Dara's hands runs a thread of purple spark, weaving between their fingers, bright against their white skin. Our eyes meet, and the spark disappears.

Gelert loudly coughs and resumes his lecture. "A Gwraig Annwn spoke to Arthur, and was so impressed with him, like, that she gave him a sword fit for a king. That was Nimuë. Some people call her the Lady of the Lake."

"And Arthur's Knights returned the sword to her when he died, through this lake," I finish.

The dog nods. "Yes . . . I think you'll find it's a bit more complicated than that. But, now it's come to you."

"But why *do I have it*? No one's given it to me," I say. "I mean, I did hear someone calling to me, kind of."

"Someone calling to you?" Dara asks.

"Yeah. That's why I'm here. I've been hearing it for two weeks."

Dara and the dog share a look that I can't decipher.

"What?" I ask.

"Err, this might be hard to get your head around," begins Dara slowly. "But you have the soul of the Lady of the Lake."

"What do you mean I *have it*?" I ask, goosebumps rising on my skin. I tap a pattern on my goose-pimpled thigh with my sword-less hand, trying to shuffle the nervous energy rushing through me.

"It's kind of like rebirth but not entirely. Like we share their spirit . . . their heart? We don't fully know the ins and outs and I don't think we ever will. It's magic."

"Magic?"

Dara nods as the words sink into my skin.

"So you're saying I *am* her?"

"Not quite. Kind of. A bit," Dara says. "It's complicated. You're her calon."

"Calon," I say, sounding it out. My stomach flips and fizzing hot anxiety rushes through me, as I try to understand what I'm being told.

"That's what we call ourselves anyway. Or what Gelert told me we do."

"How do you know it's me?"

Dara points to the sword clutched in my hands. "That's your talisman. It carries the spell that did all this. All calon have one."

A cool shiver runs down my back, and all my hair stands on end. Mumma's stories are full of talismans; magical objects that hold great power. Suddenly, I don't want to hold this sword quite as much. And yet, I can't put it down.

"How can this even be King Arthur's sword? It's the right size for me, but I'm tiny compared to like a huge warrior man," I mutter, as though the logical inconsistency will soothe the anxiety rattling my bones.

"It's magic, isn't it? Not even of this world. It doesn't have to obey the rules you know," scoffs Gelert. "Wouldn't be very useful if you couldn't lift it, would it?"

As if in agreement, the sword hums.

There's something neither of them are telling me. Growing up autistic means adults are always talking about you. Even if I didn't know what they were dancing around, I'd pick quickly up on the fact of the gap. A hole where the things they're trying not to say should be.

I've read enough stories to know that people don't just get magical ancient swords for no reason.

"So, why? What's the *point* of all this?"

Dara sighs a heavy, weary sigh. "Sorry, it's kind of hard to explain and I only know as much as Gelert's told me. But a very long time ago, a group of six witches defended our world against King Arawn of Annwn. Annwn is one of the Kingdoms of the Other. He wanted to take over our world, so they fought him and won. But the magic they used to seal him inside Annwn is wearing off, and so we, their calonnau – that's the word for all of us – are waking up."

I bark a nervous laugh as I realise what they're getting at. "So we have to stop him, is what you're saying."

"Yes, and to do that we need to find everyone, all the calonnau. It's only together that we'll have enough power to rebuild the spell that keeps him out of our world and imprisoned in his."

Hot tears prick at the corners of my eyes. This is too much. I don't want this.

"No. No, I'm not part of this *chosen one* nonsense. This could be any sword! And even if it was Excalibur, anyone could've found it! It doesn't mean anything!" I shout, my voice echoing against the mountain peaks.

My mouth is full of hot metal, and I want to scream. I struggle to my feet, yowling from the pain in my ribs, but only get halfway, crouched on my hands and knees. Dara tries to help me, but I wave them off. I don't want anyone to touch me right now, not when I'm barely holding on.

"Girl, we know because it's my job to know and find you," says the dog sharply. "Why else would we have been here at the rosy bottom of dawn? Because *I* knew you'd be here."

"You don't have to snap at me," I snap back, burying my face in my arms. "This is all just . . . too much."

"It was the water calling to you, you know. Not just the sword, although I suppose Nimuë had a hand in both. It knew you were coming."

That chill creeps up my spine again, and I don't want to listen to the truth I can feel in his words.

"Isn't every other lake in Wales *her* lake according to someone?" I groan instead.

He nudges at my arm, and I look up at him. "Some stories are true, some aren't. Most have a bit of truth to them, somewhere. The important thing is that this is the place where your sword began, and where its story ended for a bit. You were meant to find it here."

"And to find your powers," adds Dara softly.

Somehow, I know that they mean the water. Like they use light or electricity. Maybe that was why all the water stopped coming for me when I really concentrated.

But if I have magic like Dara, does that mean I have to . . . *fight* something.

This, after everything, is the thing that breaks me.

My words are gone, I know they are before I even try to speak. Dim sparks of thoughts are snuffed out before they can burn. I'm shutting down or am already there.

I have to get home.

My brain is so burned out that I can barely feel the pain, as I get up and pull my clothes right over my damp, dirty swimming things. The material of my trainers squeak as I shove my feet in.

They're talking to me, but Dara and Gelert's voices are muffled and far away, like I'm underwater. I shiver at the thought; I never want to think about water again.

Excalibur lies at their feet. I don't want it. The lake can have it back.

I pick up my rucksack and bike, and Gelert appears at my side, gently nudging his head under my arm so I can lean on him. His fur is warm and wiry, and I breathe a sigh of relief that I don't have to hold myself up.

We're moving, but I'm so dazed that I don't really know how.

The last thing I hear is Gelert. "This isn't going to go away, Vivi. Everything is about to change."

Chapter Four

The next thing I know, I'm sitting in the dirt outside my house, bike and bag at my feet. I have no idea how I got here, or where Gelert is now.

But there's no time for me to wonder: there's a light on upstairs.

I scrabble to my feet and, with the last of my energy, wheel my bike back to its place against the house and slip in through the back door.

Where I walk smack into Mam.

"Woah, hello. Good morning," she says, untangling us. She tilts her head to the side like a dog might, and her glasses slide down her nose. "Why are you so damp? And awake?"

It must still be early, but Mam is fully dressed, and her freshly washed short dark brown hair is smooth and shiny.

"Cycle," I manage to croak out. It's not a lie. I did do that . . . for a bit.

"Why?"

I shrug. My brain can't come up with lies quickly at the best of times, never mind after . . . all that.

Mam gives me a look that says *I know something is up, but I also don't have time to investigate.*

"Go have a shower. You smell ripe and, as much as I love you, I don't want you to stink out the car," she smiles.

I nod, and squeeze past her, trying to keep my face as neutral as possible so she doesn't see how in pain or close to meltdown I am.

But of course, she's my Mam. She always knows.

"Hey, what's up?" she says softly, stopping me with a hand. "Did you fall off?"

I nod because that's as good an excuse as any.

"Oh pickle," she says, kissing me on the top of my grubby forehead. "A hot bath and some quiet will help, yeah? If you need anything just shout. Mumma and I have got everything handled down here."

I wander up to the bathroom; my brain is so exhausted that it feels like time warps around me.

Climbing into the bath while not moving your ribs is actually very difficult. Once I'm finally in, I turn the dial the wrong way, like I always do, and hot water rains down on me from the showerhead. For once, I'm too tired to fix it. I plug the bath and let it rain down on me.

Heavy beads of water gather at the tip of my nose. Muck sloughs off my fingers. The water that runs off me is distinctly brown – I unplug the bath so I'm not sitting in muddy water.

Very slowly, my body starts to wake up. I move one finger at a time to see how they feel, then my toes. There's a deep ache all down my legs. My shoulders crunch as I roll them, the muscles still sore from swimming harder than I ever have before. Both my knees are scuffed pink, and the skin on my fingers looks burned raw.

My torso is bruised purple. I quietly hope my ribs aren't broken, and that this clears up quickly. I've always bruised like a peach, but this is ridiculous. There's no way the Mums won't spot this. Hopefully I can downplay the pain for a few days, until it looks less awful.

As I rub a shampoo bar over my hair, a clump of

weed falls out. Another rush of dirty water follows, and as the water turns clear again, I feel much better. A little warmth and a lot less lake go a long way.

The fuzz in my brain clears a little, and I mentally run through the next hour. Turn off water, get out of bath, get dressed, repack rucksack (currently wedged under the sink where I threw it), get in car, leave. I can do it.

It takes me a second to realise the shower has stopped running. And I didn't turn it off yet.

I pull myself up to perch on the edge of the bath and wiggle the dial – the pipes in here have always been a bit weird, but not like this.

Nothing happens.

Then I see it. Hovering above me, raining down from the showerhead, is the water: frozen in mid-air. Each drop shines like a shard of glass. It's like someone hit pause on the world, but it only worked on the shower.

The droplets look like ice, but when I touch one it's warm and yields against my skin, like a grape on the vine. I push harder, and the drop falls, turning back to normal water as it hits the plug hole.

The rest remains suspended in the air like a shimmering, near-frozen waterfall.

Is this the magic that Dara meant? Did I do this?

My attention is immediately broken by Mumma yelling from the otherwise of the door. "You done kiddo?"

At once, all the water falls to the bottom of the bath in one big boom!

I shriek, startled by the noise.

"Viv? You alright?"

"I'm fine!" I yell. "Just knocked over a bottle."

"Okay, don't be long. I need to give the bathroom a quick clean before we go."

The sound of her footsteps disappears back down the stairs, and I clamber out, wrapping myself in a fluffy towel. But now that I'm alone again, my mind turns back to the water.

I run the cold tap in the sink, and focus on the water, trying to ignore my concentrating face reflected in the tarnished silver.

I think of the sparkling purple thread of light that ran through Dara's fingers while we spoke. Could I do that with water?

I take a deep breath and try to picture myself doing it. With one eye open, I watch as, very slowly, the tap water bends towards me. And soon, it weaves through my fingers, and around my hand, still flowing down the plug hole.

They were right.

A sick feeling rises in my stomach, and I turn the tap off, rushing into the bedroom carrying my discarded clothes and backpack with me.

As I dress in dungarees and a long-sleeved t shirt, I try to push all this magic nonsense out of my mind.

Stories are one thing.

But finding out that the stories weren't ever *just* stories and were actually history? And that I'm now caught up in it all?

Nope.

Nope, nope, *nope.*

It's a relief to be in dry, warm clothes. I shove my damp swimming bits back into the box they came from, and hope nothing in there absorbs the lake smell.

The things I threw out of my rucksack are still scattered inside my bed. When I unzip it, ready to repack, I find something unexpected.

Excalibur.

The absolute last thing I want right now.

Furious, I wrap it in the jumper I was going to wear, and shove it, and everything else, into the bag.

The zips heave, but everything just about fits. I sling it on my back, whisper goodbye to my room, and stomp downstairs.

Final move preparations are in full flow. Mumma packs the last of the fridge food into our picnic bag, while Mam strides around ticking things off a big list with one of those pens you click to change the ink colour. Pushing her wild blonde hair back behind her ears, Mumma gives me a smile and hands me a breakfast bar, but luckily neither of them stop to ask why I look so terrible.

The movers arrive, and stride through our house in single file, all in identical baseball caps. They look like leaf-cutter ants, carrying our boxes into a big white van that will meet us in London.

I decide being out of the way is probably a good idea, so go out into the garden, taking one last smell of the lavender bushes. Throwing my backpack across the backseat, I ease myself into the car. Hopefully being wrapped in the jumper is good enough for the sword; the Mums would definitely ask questions if I put a seatbelt around my bag.

Headphones on, I listen to rain sounds as I watch the movers carrying our things out with ease.

I must fall asleep at some point, because soon the movers are getting into the van, and driving away.

And the Mums are outside looking at our house, their first home together, and I can tell they're saying goodbye. Mam plants a kiss on Mumma's head.

After a moment, they join me in the car. Mumma takes the driver's seat, as always. Mam settles a map on her lap, even though we all know her job is to curate the driving playlist.

"Are we all ready?" asks Mumma.

I nod, forcing a smile.

She winks at me via the wing mirror.

Mam places her hand on the window. "Bye house. Thank you for all the memories."

"Bye house," echo Mumma and I.

And with that, the car pulls away. A sob lodges in my throat, but I'm so tired that I can't even cry. I turn around to face out the back window for one final look at my first home.

Standing in the driveway is Gelert.

Everything is about to change. That's what he said, wasn't it?

I raise my hand, as if to say, 'I've seen you, but goodbye to you as well'.

He nods, but I feel like he's saying, 'I'll see you again soon.'

Maybe there really is no escaping this story.

Chapter Five

Everything is different in South London, in our little terrace house.

After one glass of dusty tap water, Mumma bought a jug that filters it and makes it taste halfway like the water from home.

Downside, more cars. Upside, no tractors, which also means no rank fertiliser being spread on the fields first thing in the morning.

Two nights in, I realise I'm missing the constant hum of sheep bleating. Instead, the passing freight trains gently rattle my windows. I'm not used to all the people sounds yet.

Down the road from us are skyscrapers and Starbucks and a shopping centre and even a cinema, things we'd normally have to drive up the coast for.

Our old farmhouse was like a witch's cottage: hung herbs drying in the kitchen, our walls decorated with drawings of plants and mushrooms, overflowing bookshelves, homemade blankets. Now all those things are inside the new, much smaller, house. Everything looks squashed in – books crammed in sideways and double stacked on the new bookshelves, plus some hidden behind the couch. The rugs that used to cover bare floorboards look a bit weird over kitchen lino and grey carpet.

A few years ago, Mam had an intense, and very short, knitting phase which kitted us out with enough blankets for a lifetime, and these are all stuffed into a wicker basket.

It all looks as out of place as I feel.

Mumma had insisted we keep most things, claiming the familiarity would help me settle in quicker, but I'm pretty sure that was an excuse for *her* to not get rid of anything.

"It'll be better once we are settled in," Mam reassures us both, over and over.

I spend the first couple of days zonked out on the couch or the bed. Luckily, the Mums think it's just from the move and don't bother me too much. Every day I unpack a few things; I don't have energy for more and my ribs still smart. Mumma helps me put up my solar system poster. Once I lay out my collection of shells, feathers, sea glass and shiny pebbles on the window sill, it looks more like *my* room.

My room looks out over everyone's back gardens, so from my bed I can watch the local cats slinking along fences, teasing dogs in their gardens.

Speaking of dogs, I keep thinking I've seen Gelert out of the corner of my eye. I catch a flash of grey, a flick of a tail, and turn, only for there to be nothing there. In the service station, at the end of our street, even in our front garden; I feel like he's haunting me. It's probably just my imagination.

I want to pretend it was all a weird dream, but my purple ribs and the sword under my bed are proof it wasn't. Poor sword; I shoved it under there and haven't looked at it again, but at night I can feel it hum softly, like it's trying to remind me that it's there.

The final bit of irrefutable proof happens on our fifth day in London, when Gelert leaps out of my wardrobe. It's such a sudden, and loud, appearance that I shriek and jump in the air, sending books and toys flying. Thank god the Mums are out.

After a pause, he says, "Well, then. Hello to you too."

Before I can respond, my tablet, which I had been using just before his arrival, slides off the bed and lands with a final thud.

"Oh," he says, giving it a rude look.

My racing heart slows and is replaced with a sinking feeling.

"It's very rude to barge in on people unannounced, you know," I huff, gathering my things back up.

Gelert sniffs at my windowsill nature collection. "Can hardly ring the doorbell, can I?"

"How did you even find me?" I mutter, as he noses around my bedroom.

"I know your address," he says, like this isn't absolutely ludicrous.

"What, like you googled *Vivi Conway new house*?"

"No, that would be ridiculous," he snorts. "It was on all those boxes in your old house."

I scrunch up my nose. "Wait, you can read?"

The dog stares at me like I'm the silliest thing he's ever seen. "Of course I can read, girl."

"Teach you that in puppy class did they? Sit, stay, write a book report.'

"Don't be daft, girl. Puppies can't read." With a big

48

huff, he sends a barn owl feather floating into the air.

"Why do all conversations with you feel like riddles?" I rub at my eyes and sit back down on the bed.

This is worse than talking to non-autistic people. There's always a layer of something I'm missing with them, like I'm not fluent in their language. Everyone else grew up fluently speaking "person" and I'm still fumbling with the basic phrases.

But with Gelert, it's another level.

He stretches out his great long legs and settles on the patterned blue and gold rug in the middle of my floor. "I'll make it easy for you − yes, I can read. No, other dogs can't read. But I'm not a normal dog."

"You can say that again," I mutter.

"Plus, I followed you, like."

So, it *was* him I keep seeing. He's known where I was the whole time.

"It's not my fault I don't know what you can do," I say a little sulkily. "You could have been just a normal illiterate dog with no magic.

We stare at each other for a moment, and he blinks slowly at me, before carrying on.

"Alright, fair. But stop expecting magical things to behave by non-magical rules. I was a normal dog, a long time ago. There's a lot you can do in a thousand years, *including* learn to read."

A thousand years? No wonder he's grumpy.

"Wait. Are you super old or . . . You're a ghost?"

"There we are, you got there eventually! Dda iawn."

"I've never met a ghost before."

"Oh tidy, I'm glad the whole purpose of my afterlife has been—".

"Alright, alright," I say, cutting him off before he can say something that will annoy me again. "So, why have you been stalking me?"

"I'm not stalking you."

"Just a light haunting then."

"I'm keeping an eye on you, aren't I? For your own good might I add."

"Wow, that doesn't sound sinister at all."

He stares at me for an uncomfortably long time, clearly annoyed with me for being difficult. "You've still got the sword, I hope?"

I lift my mattress and retrieve Excalibur from its hiding place. As my hand wraps around the hilt, it hums a little 'thank you'. I lay it on the duvet, and it looks so out of place next to my plush bunnies.

"Is part of keeping an eye on me convincing me to

help Dara?"

"Something like that, aye."

"This was supposed to be my fresh start," I groan. "I just wanted an easy quiet life."

"Sounds dull."

"Maybe, but it's safe. No monsters, no new people, no annoying ghost dogs."

The words hang in the air between us.

"Not that I want to tell you what to do," he begins, which I interrupt with a barked laugh. "But you know Nimuë also struggled with the decision to fight against him too."

"I'm not her," I mutter.

"You look like her when you scowl."

"I don't scowl," I say, hurriedly rearranging my face.

"You always were stubborn as a mule," he laughs softly.

"I'm not her, don't you get it?" I yell far too loudly, all patience gone down the drain.

He falters and shrinks into himself, and I feel immediately guilty. For a dog as tall as me, he seems suddenly very small. His eyes are glassy, faraway.

"I'm sorry Gelert. I didn't mean to shout," I plead, my voice crumbly and tired. "There's too much new.

I can't keep up with it all."

I hate admitting how hard things can be, especially to a person I don't know. Or dog, I guess. I like dogs but part of the appeal is that they don't talk back, and Gelert seems almost halfway between a dog and a person.

"Is moving that terrible? You fought an afanc after all. That's no mean feat." He doesn't say it unkindly; it's almost encouraging. But the thing is, that's not how autism works. People always think that because I can do one thing, I must be able to do something else that they think is equally no big deal, though to me the two things don't remotely compare. Or worse, they act like I'm making a big deal out of nothing. But they don't know what it's like for me, really.

"It's different for me. I'm autistic," I begin, realising that a thousand-year-old ghost dog probably has no idea what that means. "It means my brain is wired differently. I find lots of stuff really difficult to do on a good day, but especially when things change. And this week, there's been lots and lots of changes, and they all pile up and my brain slows down because I'm still processing it all. I get anxious when I don't know what is going to happen, and because everything is different, I can't predict anything. And then you're trying to add a whole new . . . reality on top of it all."

Gelert is quiet for some time, his eyes trained on his paws. After a moment, he gets to his feet. "Alright, we'll go at your pace."

"Thank you,' I say, lying down on the bed. "I'm still wrapping my head around the idea that magic is real, and not just from stories. Like, I always kind of hoped it was real, but that's different from knowing."

"The thing is, there are whole worlds of magic around you all the time. Just like galaxies," he says, looking at the poster on my wall. "Some you can see; some you haven't found yet. Not being able to see them doesn't make them less real, does it?"

"Astronomy's another hobby of yours?"

"Something like that. There's lots to learn from this internet of yours. Dara does the scrolling for me; it's a bit difficult with paws," he says. "Speaking of magic, how's yours coming along?"

While I don't want to admit it, I have been practicing a little. Water bends to me now and it's getting easier. I can stop water running from the taps without much thought, though I have to remember to actually turn it off or it eventually starts running again, and Mam gets annoyed about wasted water. I'm also a whizz at stirring milk into my tea.

"Pretty okay," I admit.

"Good," he says. "Keep practicing. I know all this is big, but it'll feel worse if you keep holding it at arm's length."

I kind of hate that I know he's right.

"And talk to Nimuë. She'll help you make sense of it all. Alright, I'll be off then, shall I?"

"Wait! What do you mean talk to her? How?"

"The sword," he says. "The talisman connects you to her."

"What, like a phone?" An extremely sharp phone . . .

"No not like a phone," he sniffs.

"But isn't she dead? Or like, part of me?"

The front door opens downstairs and the Mums clatter back into the house.

"I'll come again," Gelert says, disappearing on the spot. Evidently, the wardrobe was just a prop for dramatics.

I go downstairs and help them unload the shopping. But later that night, while I'm tucked up in bed, I think about magic.

If there's so much out there, it can't just be me and

Dara who know about it.

Googling *is magic real?* gives me a lot of very strange results. An article about covens of witches throughout Scotland, a scientific essay about the psychology of people who believe in magic, and a Wikipedia article called "magic (supernatural)".

I'm not really sure what I was hoping to find, but this isn't it.

I try a few more, ending with *weird magic things happening in Britain*, but before I can read any results, I fall asleep.

Chapter Six

The first day of school comes around too quickly. I end up not starting the same day as everyone else; the Mums decided I needed more time to settle in before starting somewhere new. So, it isn't until a Friday in mid-September that I find myself standing in reception.

I'd been allowed to come look around and meet my teachers with the Mums before the term started, but it was weird being in such a big empty building.

Today, it's filled with students, and everyone seems to know where they are going.

I was told to wait in reception for someone to take me to my first class, and so I do, clutching the straps of my backpack. In order to feel less like a lemon, I look at the photos of concerts and competitions and former students on the wall.

"Are you Vivi Conway?" asks a bright, high voice.

"Yeah, I am," I croak.

"Nice!" says a friendly looking girl. Her dark hair is braided, with little coloured beads at the ends. The bright red school uniform jumper shines against her deep brown skin. "I'm Chiasoka Emezi. We're in the same form class, so Mr. Reynolds said I should come show you around, yeah?"

"Oh, thanks," I say, following her past displays of artwork.

"So where did you move from?"

"North Wales."

"Omg!" she shouts, pronouncing it *ohh emm gee*. "I figured you just moved from another bit of London. That's cool. I bet it's very different?"

"Yeah, just a bit."

She laughs, but not *at* me. There's a difference. "It can be intense here, but the people are nice. Or like, most of them anyways."

"Were you in any clubs at your old school?" But she continues before I can answer. "We have a few here. I'm in choir, and I've been begging for a drama club, but no luck yet. Can you sing?"

Words bounce out of her, lilting and bright and full of wonder.

I think back to the lake, when being able to sing might have come in useful. "Unfortunately, not at all."

"Oh, I'm sure you're not that bad. Everyone can sing, especially with a bit of practice and training. Practice makes perfect," she trills the last line.

"Yeah, no. I'm pretty sure I'm unteachable. Best I don't inflict my wailing on everyone."

"Haha, okay okay, that's fine with me. I'm just glad you're not a soloist; I don't need any more competition."

"You sing a lot?"

"Yeah, and, no lie, I'm really good." If literally anyone else said this, I might think they were a bit big-headed, but there's something so easily confident about Chiasoka that I just believe her.

"We always need more audience members. You'll come watch us sing, yeah? We always do a big performance at Christmas."

"Um, sure?"

"Yay! I knew I had a good feeling about you, Vivi Conway," she says, and all at the same time

I feel happy and like my stomach is full of bees. "Mr. Reynolds will probably make you join the Science Club, FYI."

"Science Club?" I say, trying to play it cool, but inside I'm really excited.

"Yeah, it's his baby. My mum's a doctor so she always makes me sign up, but the upside is there's always pretty good trips. We're going to the Science Museum on Monday, so you should make sure you can go!"

"Okay," I say, genuinely excited. I've never been to the Science Museum but I've always wanted to go. It's on the list of Pros about moving to London that we made over the summer.

"Wait!" she says, stopping to look at me closely. "Your eyes! They're so beautiful."

"Oh, thanks, Chiasoka."

It's slightly ironic that for a person who is terrible at eye contact, my eyes are often the first thing people notice. One is dark brown, the other mossy green.

"You can call me Chia, if you want."

I nod, giving her a small smile.

Chia stops in her tracks. "Do you like to read?"

"Err, yeah?"

"Me too! Did they show you the library?"

I shake my head, and she opens what looks like a door to a supply closet. It's small but definitely a library. Shelves are stacked with books with coloured dots on their spines, and there are a couple of very worn-in chairs. The air smells musty with old pages.

When I look back at Chia, she's kneeling in front of the table, comparing two sheets of paper. "I think we both have all the same classes and lunches."

Before I can say anything, she starts underlining all the room names and numbers in sparkly gel pen, a kind of colour-coding that will hopefully become clear to me eventually. The yellow pen she uncaps smells strongly of fake not-quite bananas.

Everything is fine, and then suddenly, I'm hit with a tidal wave of Bad Thoughts. *Kelly Keane used to help you out*, it says. *Until she had enough of you and made new friends. Started noticing the parts of you she could prod and laugh at, without pushing you so far that you'd tell a teacher.* My palms are sweaty, and I want to get out of here.

But, before I can, Chia stands up and hands me the sheet. "Here you go. Anyway, I come here a lot and read, so you should come here too. It's nice and quiet. I figure you might like that."

The Bad Thoughts are replaced by a different kind of unease wobbling in my stomach. "Why would you think that?" I ask quietly.

She looks up from her schedule, nonplussed. "Because you're autistic, right?"

My mouth falls open. I don't know what to say, but I feel a bit weird about her working it out so quickly.

"My older sister is autistic too," she explains, and putting the sheets under one arm. "And I speak BSL." She signs as she speaks out loud. "I think your Mums must have told the school that, so they asked me to help you out."

Relief floods through me. I know a bit of BSL; very useful for when I can't will my tongue to move.

"I won't tell anyone unless you specifically tell me to. Ife – that's my sister – always gets upset if people just introduce her as 'the autistic one' without asking if she wants them to know. Ruuuuuuude."

I know I had planned to not make any new friends if I could help it, but maybe Chia is alright. She seems nice, and I don't feel like I need to second-guess what she's saying.

I follow Chia up to our form class, which is in one of the Science rooms. The beads in her hair chime as we walk.

Mr. Reynolds sits behind the desk, drinking a huge cup of coffee – I already met him the other day. He's a very tall man with a relaxed vibe, and I liked him straight away. I'd always gotten on pretty well with teachers, probably much better than with people my own age.

"Vivi, welcome," he beams. "You all ready for your first day?"

I nod, my words drying up already. My mouth feels as dry as the desert. I'm so out of practice with talking to people. This morning, I've had more non-parent human interactions than I've had in months.

Clearly sensing what's going on, Chia turns to me and signs along with Mr. Reynolds' words for me.

"Chia is going to be your buddy this week, help you with your classes and everything. She knows this school almost as well as I do."

She gives me a reassuring smile.

"If you guys have any problems, you can just come back to me. That cool with you?" he says. Normally, I'd cringe at a teacher saying *cool* to me, but Mr. Reynolds is kind of cool. So, I guess it's okay.

I give him a thumbs up, and immediately regret it.

Definitely *not* cool.

"And I hope you'll consider joining the Science Club?"

"Please!" I manage to croak.

"Vivi will need the permission forms so she can come with us to the Science Museum, Mr Reynolds," Chia says.

"Good thinking! I'll email them and all the info to your Mum now and let her know you might want to stay for Science Club after school," he says. "I know it's your first day, so a lot's going on, but if you make it later, I can tell you more about the trip so you can decide if you're up for it. Cool?"

"Cool," I say.

The day is a total blur, and I'm thankful that Chia is in charge of me. I would definitely have gotten lost without her. The classrooms are so far apart that we have to walk the whole length of the school between some of our lessons.

When the bell rings for the end of school, Chia leads me back up to our form class for Science Club.

The classroom is totally empty, but Chia strides in and I just have to hope that this is allowed. I follow her in and sit down next to her. Her gel pens are back out, and she's filling out her homework diary.

Mr. Reynolds pops in and says he'll be back to start shortly. He hands me a printed sheet about the trip to the Science Museum before disappearing again, leaving another huge coffee on his desk.

I'm just about to read when I hear my name being called.

In the doorway, looking kind of glamorous with their hair shaved at the sides, glossily long on top, is Dara.

Chapter Seven

There's no sparkling electricity running over their fingers, no ghost dog, but the person before me is unmistakably Dara. The person who saved my life, and who now needs my help.

Social anxiety is the least of my problems when there's a reminder of my magical destiny standing right there in the doorway.

We lock eyes as they walk over to me.

"It *is* you," they whisper, sitting down on the other side of me.

"What . . . are you doing here?" I whisper, stumbling over my words.

"This is my school?" Suddenly, Dara begins to laugh. "Oh my days. *Of course* we'd end up finding each other again."

"You two know each other already?" Chia asks, clicking on the lid of a bright green pen that smells of mint.

"Oh . . . yeah, we met in the park the other day," says Dara.

"Dara and me were in primary school together," Chia adds. Thankfully she gets up to leave. "I'm just going to go to the loo."

"What a coincidence huh?" Dara laughs.

"This is really your school?"

"Unless I've successfully implanted false memories in Chia, it must be. This is fate, or magic I guess."

It turns out that we even live right by each other – Dara's house is a few streets over, by the Polish corner shop and ominous playground.

"I'm guessing Gelert's been to see you?"

"Oh yeah," I groan. "Does he live with you?"

"No, he doesn't. When he comes round, my little dog Cally always freaks out, like she *knows* he's there. I don't know where he goes the rest of the time. Have you been practicing?"

"Practicing what?" Chia returns to her seat, possibly the fastest loo trip in the world.

"Her . . . her cartwheels!"

"Cartwheels." I repeat. I have never done a cartwheel. I have never come even slightly close to being able to do a cartwheel.

"Oh, we've got gymnastics in PE this term, so that'll be useful," says Chia.

"Yes . . . Dara was teaching me how to do them," I add, completely unconvincingly.

A girl with long shiny black hair appears at the door and barks a laugh. "You need a new teacher. Dara has the grace of a bulldozer."

"Omg, as if the first thing you say is mean," says Chia, laughing.

I kick Dara's booted foot under the table. "Not at school," I hiss, hoping they don't think I'm just really weird about cartwheels.

"Anyway, new person, you're in my spot," the girl says flatly.

"Don't be rude," Chia says, not looking up from her writing.

"I always sit there."

"Vivi is new. She can sit where she likes. But if you're going to be cranky, I'll shift over," says Chia, sliding her things along a space. "Cranky-pants here is Stevie Lin"

"I'm not cranky," Stevie grumbles, while taking Chia's vacated seat.

Just as I'm about to brave a hi, she says "Vivi, is it?"

I nod, the words dead on my tongue.

"And you're new here?"

I nod again.

"Chatty, aren't you?" she says with a shark grin.

"Put the claws away, Stevie. Be nice," says Chia firmly, pointing at her with a grape-scented purple pen.

Stevie slips off her rucksack and adjusts the sleeve of her jumper on her left arm, which ends just below the elbow. "I am nice!"

Dara snorts, while Chia says "Of course," patting Stevie on the back.

"I am!" she snaps.

I cannot get a read on Stevie. She's spiky. A little like Danielle, Kelly's new best friend. I swallow hard, trying not to think about that similarity.

"Look, I'm not going to bite you. Unless you give me a reason to," Stevie says to me. She's so matter of fact that I can't tell if she's joking.

More people file in, and so does Mr. Reynolds, returning to his giant tureen of coffee.

"I hope you're all excited for our first Discovery Day on Monday!" he says with a huge grin. "Once a month, as part of your scientific education, we'll go out on a research trip. It won't always be a big museum, but I promise it'll always be educational and fun!"

"Are we just looking at stuff?" groans Hari, a boy I recognise from one of my classes earlier.

"Not just looking Hari, don't you worry. Tour guides are going to take us round the Climate Change and Weather exhibits, but we'll be doing some fun hands-on stuff while we're there!"

Mr. Reynolds starts going through the list of who has handed in their permission slips, and I know I should probably pay attention, but meeting Dara again, and whatever that was with Stevie, has undeniably rattled me.

An anxious buzzing builds in my head, so I breathe slowly, and I flick my fingers, hoping to shift the energy. Even though I'm trying not to pay attention to her, I know that Stevie is watching me out of the corner of her eye, which makes everything worse.

Needing something to do with my hands, I fumble for my water bottle. As I unscrew the lid, I twitch and the bottle slips. A plume of water fountains into the air right towards Stevie, whose eyes widen with expectation.

Oh no.

Come back, I think desperately.

Stevie screams, leaping up.

But she's bone dry. And my bottle is full.

"Stevie?" asks Mr. Reynolds. "You alright?"

All eyes are on her, except mine which bore directly into the table.

"Thought I saw a spider," she says coolly, sitting down as though nothing happened. She flicks her long hair over a shoulder.

"September is spider season," says Mr. Reynolds. "They'll be coming inside to keep warm. Keep an eye out for their lovely webs!"

Everything seems really amazing all the time to Mr. Reynolds.

"Wonderful," she mutters, and I get the impression she actually *is* afraid of spiders.

I screw the cap onto my bottle without looking up.

"Weird. I could've sworn you were just about to soak me," Stevie says under her breath.

I look down at my feet, hoping the floor might swallow me, and in the gap between our stools lie three tell-tale drops of water.

My hopes that no one would pay me any attention here are totally dashed. In one day, I've gained someone who could be a genuine friend, an enemy, and someone determined that I'm going to help them save the world.

This fresh start is not going well.

Chapter Eight

I'm exhausted by everything today.

When Mr. Reynolds calls time at the end of Science Club, I grab my stuff and pace home. I know that someone, probably Chia, calls after me, but I'm so low on energy that I can't stop to talk or I'm going to cry.

I quite like the walk, it turns out. Normally Mumma would have to pick me up as we lived so far away from school, but here I'm only a few streets away.

The roads are wide, and tree lined. The chicken shop at the end of the road smells so delicious that I slow down just to take it in. I pass a pharmacy with posters in the window that must be as old as my Mums, a couple of little shops, and a bakery with fresh bread in the window.

There's a lot of new here, but it's distracting in a nice way for once.

Mumma is in the garden as I get back and waves a trowel at me in hello.

But, as I close the gate and turn round to say hello properly, I freeze.

Learning against the front door is Dara.

"I've just been meeting your lovely new friend," Mumma beams, as she repots some plants using the closed lids of the wheelie bins as a table.

"And I've been meeting your lovely mum," says Dara, smooth as anything.

They laugh like old friends, and I grit my teeth.

"Dara says they promised to show you around," Mumma says, and I can't ignore how much she's glowing. I can't blame her for being excited that I've made a friend after everything that happened last year, even if Dara is technically more like a co-worker I didn't want.

"Uh huh," I concede.

"Why don't you stay for dinner?" Mumma asks Dara, and I have to force myself not to yell *NO*.

"That's very kind of you, Mrs. Conway. Maybe another time? I would love to come in for a bit to get to know Vivi better, if that's alright?"

I give the least enthusiastic thumbs up I can possibly muster.

"Of course!" Mumma whips off her gloves and bustles inside. "Hot chocolates? What milk do you drink? Are you vegan?" She fires out a million questions which Dara answers dutifully – yes, any, no – while we undo our shoes.

"Aren't you afraid of going to a stranger's house?" I ask, leading them upstairs so we can talk without Mumma overhearing.

"Vee, I can shoot electricity out of my hands. There's not much about normal life that freaks me out any more."

I push the door open wearily, and almost leap out of the room in shock. There's something in there. Something huge on my bed.

"What is it?" Dara charges in, purple light shimmering around them.

But it's luckily not a monster. It's more annoying than that. Napping in a patch of sunlight on my duvet is Gelert.

"Oh, hiya Gelert," says Dara, dropping their hands.

"Make yourself at home why don't you?" I say to

him, willing my heart to slow down.

With a great yawn and a stretch, he says, "Aye I did, thanks."

"Ooh, big stretch." Dara scratches behind Gelert's ears and it must be a good one because he shuts his eyes.

"Don't patronise me," he murmurs, eyes still closed.

Gelert doesn't move to get off the bed, which he takes up most of, so Dara and I settle on the rug.

"Nice room," they say, wrestling with their enormous rucksack. "It's so weird that we're at the same school and live so close. I wonder if the magic is like bringing us together. Perhaps it's part of the spell."

"The sword is doing something," growls Gelert.

Under the mattress, I find it humming, gently vibrating through the covers. I remove it, and both the sword and Gelert seem to settle down quickly.

Meanwhile, with a huge thump, Dara deposits a huge folder onto the floor in front of me. It's bursting at the seams, and bits of paper stick out at odd angles.

I'm just about to ask what it is when Mumma barges through the door yelling, "Treat time!"

Thankfully, Gelert has vanished.

"Thank you, Abigail." Of course Dara already

knows her name.

Mumma sets two steaming cups of hot chocolate down on my desk, but as she turns round her face falls. "Erm, why do you have a sword Vivi?"

My stomach drops and I'm about to fall into a spiral of spluttering.

But Dara casually says, "It's a prop from school. I really want to do a play about King Arthur, and Vivi heard about it, so we're talking through ideas."

I can only assume Dara also has psychic powers, because Mumma loves theatre. They have unknowingly said the magic words, and I know she desperately wants to ask us about it but is trying to be a parent.

"I'll leave you to it!" she squeaks, closing the door behind her.

"That was much better than the cartwheel lie," I say a little too sharply.

"Sorry about that. I didn't think I'd find you at school, so hadn't thought about a cover story."

"Why *did* you pick cartwheels?"

They shrug. "I dunno, I just really wish I could do one."

Lying has never come easy to me, and I hate it when other people do it just to save my feelings.

I prefer the truth, or at least, I think I do. Glancing down at the folder, I'm not so sure any more.

"So, what is this?

"Our cover story," they say with an enormous grin. "I don't know about your parents, but mine notice when I get fixated on a new thing and like to ask questions. So, I pretended that I'm writing a play. Except it's pretty much all research about the calonnau and talismans and stuff."

Dara flicks through the folder slowly. The start is all about the technicalities of staging a play; sketches of costumes and scribbled notes. Then, they flick to the middle and it's all about us. Gelert. A map of North Wales with a big red circle around my valley. Notes about the weather. Excalibur.

"This is kind of genius."

"Well, I am kind of a genius," Dara laughs.

"Wait, what happens if someone wants to see what you've been working on?"

"I'll insist that it needs more time. And if they get twitchy, I'll perform something *so* terrible that they never ask about it again."

Gelert reappears on the bed. "That won't be a challenge; I've seen your homework."

Dara sticks out their tongue at him. "Rude."

"Could you not have taken the sword with you?" I ask him.

He looks at me for a few beats then simply says "No." I'm pretty sure he says it just to be extra annoying.

Dara passes me one of the hot chocolates. It's perfect drinking temperature. The marshmallows have melted into a singular gooey mass.

Holding it between both hands, I take a sip. When I set it down on the floor, I realise I've been slowly mixing it with my magic.

"Nice work," says Dara.

"It's just stirring."

"Sure, but you also moved a bottle's worth of water earlier. Oh my days, I thought Stevie was going to carve you up."

"You saw?"

"Of course."

"Why didn't you say anything?"

"I didn't want her to realise there were other witnesses. Hopefully she just thinks it was a trick of the light."

"I'm not so sure about that."

"Hey, don't worry about it," they say, taking a sip of

their hot chocolate. "First few weeks I was constantly making our lightbulbs explode. Pops thought our wiring was faulty and had to get an electrician out."

I go back to the folder, and on a clean page Dara has started a list. At the top it says: 1. Ceridwen: Dara, electricity, awl.

"What's an awl?" I ask.

From their jacket, Dara pulls out a small tool and holds it in the flat of their palm. It's long and pointed at one end, with a rounded handle at the other.

"It's like an early multi-tool. Good for poking holes in leather or wood, you know, hard stuff. And you can tighten screws, engrave things, even break stuff. Like an ancient Swiss Army knife."

"And yours is magical?" I ask.

"I don't really know much about it yet, honestly," they say, turning it over in their hand. "I know it belonged to Ceridwen, who is my calon, but I haven't spoken to her yet. I don't really know what it meant for her."

"What do you mean?"

"Well, for you, Nimuë gave that sword to Arthur right? And then it was given back to her. It's part of her story."

"Oh, I see," I say, not really seeing.

"Anyway, not all of us are going to get an enchanted sword, are they?"

My cheeks flush, but they break into a grin and we both laugh.

"What was Ceridwen like?" Her name is familiar to me, but I can't place her.

Dara flips to a printed-out painting of a woman wearing a red dress and a very pleased-with-herself smile. Next to her is a cauldron.

"Pagans worship her as the goddess of inspiration, and she was also a maker. She used to build enchanted objects like this cauldron, so it kind of follows that my talisman is a tool. I think she's most famous for making a weird knowledge spell for her son, but it went totally wrong."

I look at Gelert, expecting him to fill in the details, but he doesn't add anything.

"I'm still new to this, so I guess I'll find out why one day. When she speaks to me finally," Dara adds.

"What about the cauldron?" I ask.

"You'll find a blinking great cauldron is little less portable," Gelert finally pipes up. "It was tricksy too. Had a terrible habit of transforming people into things if they used it at the wrong time of year."

"Oh, that doesn't sound ideal."

"Also, people kept thinking it was the Holy Grail and going on pilgrimages to find it."

"And did they?"

"Not yet."

Dara pulls out a pen, and underneath the first line of their list they write: 2. Nimuë: Vivi, water, Excalibur.

"Do you know anything about the other four yet?"

To my surprise, Gelert huffs.

Dara leans in and whispers, "Gelert doesn't know who they are."

"I do know," he says haughtily. "I just can't . . . remember. They are two very different things."

"Sorry Gel," says Dara, scratching the dog's haunch.

"How did you find me then?" I ask.

"When the magic gathers around a calon and they're going to get their powers, it changes the atmosphere. Like, there'll be some really weird weather. Before I got my powers, we had this muggy and hot weather that meant we had thunderstorms basically every night. It was properly weird, like people on the tv talked about it weird."

"How did you get yours?" I interrupt.

"So, I'd gone mudlarking—"

"Mud what?"

"Like, treasure hunting! But along rivers!"

I pull a face at this.

"No really, it's so cool. Along the Thames you can find lots of old stuff like coins and bones. Mum had made Rabbie, my older brother, take me to this meet up, though he was on the phone to his girlfriend of the week. I had this feeling, like my hand was being directed, and it was just there in the mud."

"That sounds significantly easier than how I found mine," I say, thinking of the afanc and the near drowning.

"I mean, a bunch of these nasty little cobber fellas turned up and tried to steal it."

"Coblyns," Gelert corrects.

"Yes, coblyns. Like a nasty little garden gnome with really big teeth. Horrible things. I got a few zaps in by accident, but I mostly just kicked them off and told Rabbie it was time to go. I guess they can't easily chase after a London bus. Not been able to look at a garden gnome the same since." They pull a face, and we both laugh.

"When did you two meet then?"

"He was in my room when I got home that day."

"Oh, so this is a habit of yours?" I say to the dog, who humphs at me.

"Anyway! The point is that there was that bit of weird weather beforehand."

"And we had rain and flooding . . ." I murmur.

"Exactly. Managed to narrow down the area thanks to Google Maps and the local news, and then when we saw the lake Gelert remembered Nimuë and knew we had to go there."

"How did you even get there?"

"Gelert just whizzed me there. Like, it's not teleportation, but it's not *not* teleportation."

"Wait, is that how I got home? Did you carry me?"

"I'm not a flipping donkey," he sniffs, evidently uninterested in making things clearer.

"Is this how you can just appear whenever?" I prod.

"It is," answers Dara, when the dog only snores in return. "He can take us with him, but not for long. The journey to your lake from here was a big one for him. It's why he's so tired out now."

I feel a little bit bad about an ancient ghost dog being this exhausted because of me.

"That's pretty much everything I know so far," says Dara. "We've got a lot to still work out, but another day."

I'm relieved to hear this. I just want to curl up on my bed and fall asleep like Gelert.

"Hey, let's hang out tomorrow. There's a cool park I can show you. I'll give your Mums directions," they say, and before I can reply they're already downstairs.

"Are you going too?" I ask Gelert, still reclined on my bed.

He raises one hairy eyebrow at me, and sighs. "If I must."

And in a puff of smoke, he's gone too.

It's only after they're gone that I realise that I was so caught up in finding out about what happened to Dara, and what they knew, that I didn't tell them I didn't want to be involved. In a way, I just went along with everything, letting Dara write me into their gigantic guide of looming destiny.

Not that I really have a choice about any of it.

I'm snapped out of my moping when Mam, fresh from work in a sapphire suit, knocks on my door. She perches next to me on the bed and smooths back my wild hair. "How was your first day?"

I make a noise that's somewhere between a *mmm* and an *ehhh*.

"I heard you made a nice new friend and joined the Science Club. That's really good work Vivi. I'm so proud of you." She must see how exhausted I am because she adds, "It'll get easier."

"Mmm-hmm. Did you have a good first day at work?" I croak.

"Mmm-hmm," she groans with the exact same intonation.

"I hear it gets easier."

She pulls a face at me. "Alright smartie. Look, I know it's scary and tiring, but it's good to have people you love and trust in your life. We're social creatures. We need people."

"Do we?" I say. It's supposed to be jokey, but it comes out all wrong. Bitter like orange pith, and scared. I feel nauseous at the thought of needing people

Mam rubs her thumb slowly over my forehead, like when I have a headache. "You'll find your people, who love you for who you are. It sounds like Dara's pretty keen on you."

My mind flashes to Dara and Chia. Gelert too, maybe. Stevie, not quite so much. Mam doesn't get what it's like to be me, to be a kid right now, but

I dunno. She's smart. Maybe she's right about this. Maybe I'm just being scared because of what happened before.

I nod and give her a brave smile.

"And, if anyone gives you a hard time, I'll set Mumma on them," she says, flashing her eyes.

She pulls me into her arms as we laugh, and she squeezes me tightly. "Come on, let's go have dinner. Plus, your Mumma wants to know how your day went, and she'll explode if we leave her any longer."

After dinner of meatballs and a heavily edited version of my day told to my Mums, I decide to go lie in bed early. I'm overstimulated still, so I turn out the big light, draw the curtains and put on my night-light. It projects stars onto the ceiling. I watch it quietly for a little while, and soon my mind drifts to that conversation with Gelert about all the different types of magic.

I grab my tablet, and realise I never looked the results for *weird magic things happening in Britain*. Luckily, the tab is still open.

The top result is a website called *Strange Britain*, which I click onto without thinking.

The i's in Britain in the title are replaced by

magnifying glasses.

It's kind of a blog; people write in with questions like *how can I get ceremonial wine stains out of my carpet* and *has anyone seen a shadow like this before* and *how do you tell pixies from nixies*, which are all answered by someone called the Ghost Queen. Presumably the person who runs the website.

I'm not really reading anything in depth, but it does make me wonder . . . Does that mean there are other people who might know about us and this spell? And if so, what does that mean for us?

I close the browser and shut the tablet just to be safe; that's enough magic for today.

Chapter Nine

I'm standing by the edge of a lake.

The last thing I remember is lying on my bed.

I don't know how I got here.

Wherever here is.

Floating in the air are tiny glowing lights, illuminating the gloom. They remind me of bioluminescence in the sea – tiny creatures who light up at night.

Lilac-grey fog thickens the air; I can only see a little way ahead of me and all that is just flat, silvery water.

Echoing around me is a drip, drip, drip, like a leaky tap dropping into a full bath. Also like a bath, the water steams ever so slightly.

But when I dip a toe in, the water is ice cold.

"Hello?" My voice echoes like I've shouted into

a cave. "Is anyone there? Gelert?"

"Hello." A voice like velvet replies.

I freeze. It's definitely not Gelert.

"Hello? Can you help me? I think I'm lost. Or dreaming. Quite possibly both."

A ripple forms on the surface of the water. There's something in there.

I leap back; I've learned my lesson. The last thing that came out of a lake wasn't exactly friendly.

What appears is not an afanc.

It's a woman, dressed in a silver-green dress that shimmers with the water. Her long, tangled hair is the rich grey of angry waves in a storm.

"Vivian," she purrs.

It's not a question. She knows who I am.

"Vivi," I answer, standing straight.

"Vivi," she whispers, stretching the sounds in my name out melodically. "Viiiivvvviiii."

I'm not sure if she's speaking to me or practicing my name.

"Do not be afraid Vivi."

"I'm not," I lie.

She smiles and walks slowly towards me. Her dress and hair float, like the air is water. Even though she's right in front of me, everything looks a little too soft, like an out-of-focus picture.

"Who are you?"

I brace as she slowly raises a hand and touches the centre of my chest with one long bone-white finger.

"We're the same," she breathes. "We have the same heart."

"No offence ma'am, but you and I don't even look alike," I say.

She laughs like a wind chime in the breeze.

And I realise what she means. "Wait, are you—"

"Nimuë," she says, moving to place the same hand over her own heart.

My calon, or am I her calon? Maybe it applies both ways. I should ask Gelert which it is . . . if it matters. Is the grammar that important? (My teachers would probably say yes.)

"I should've seen that coming, shouldn't I? With the lake and the general magical vibes."

"Our lake," she corrects, and I realise what she means as the fog lifts slightly.

The mountains are deep bruised blurs in the distance, but I know we're at my lake, the lake where all of this began. It's the same place, even if it's now purple and glowy . . . somehow.

I slump down onto the moss-thick grass. "Are you here to give me the talk about accepting my role in this prophecy or whatever, because the dog already gave it a go."

She glides down elegantly and sits next to me. How we are related I do not know . . . if related is even the right word. I can't move without falling into things, whereas she basically floats.

"I'm not here to convince you of anything, Vivi. I just wanted to talk to you."

"So, I'm asleep? And we're talking through the sword somehow."

"The sword connects us, in a way. As do all the talismans. They reach across time and space, thanks to a sprinkle of magic."

"I don't mean to be blunt, but aren't you dead?"

"A little."

A very normal answer. I'm unfortunately getting used to these kinds of cryptic responses. Perhaps it *is* a rule that ghost-dogs and ghost-humans can only speak in riddles.

"And I used to think you could only be totally dead or not at all," I groan.

91

A twinkle of laughter again.

"My body is dead, yes. But my spirit lives on in you. Through the power of dreams, we can reach across time and speak as though we are side by side."

"So, you're . . . inside me?"

She tilts her head from side to side. "It is hard to explain simply. Our souls are entwined. We are separate and the same. Magic binds us together. We are each other's calon."

Clear as mud. But at least she answered my grammar question.

"I've been waiting a very long time to meet you," she says.

"Did you know it would be me?"

"No, just that I would recognise you."

"I didn't ask for this to happen." It comes out quiet, sulky.

"No, you did not. And I'm sorry for that." Her storm blue eyes shine with tears, and she runs her fingers through her hair, over and over. I feel slightly bad for saying it. "It is unfair that we made a willing sacrifice of ourselves, and you were denied that choice. But you were chosen."

We sit quietly for some time, and I wonder about

telling her I'm autistic and that I sometimes struggle with communication. I don't think I have a script for "small talk by the side of a magical waterway with the Lady of the Lake." I mean, given that we're apparently the same, maybe she'll just get it.

"How did it end up being me and Dara . . . and whoever else?"

"In truth, I do not know the intricacies of the spell. We all had different roles. In this, I just offered my power. The spell itself was designed by Ceridwen. A kind of scrying spell, one that would lie dormant until—"

"Arawn started to get free?"

"Yes. It would activate the talismans and summon our calonnau to them. And we scattered them around, just in case."

She doesn't elaborate in case of what, and frankly I don't want to ask.

"Ceridwen is Dara's calon," I say and Nimuë nods. "They found the awl in the Thames."

Nimuë laughs, shaking her head. "We threw that into the sea from Orkney. It must have washed the whole way there, determined to find them." Her white teeth bite softly into her plump lips. We look so very different, but we stim the same. Maybe this is what Gelert could see when he said I was like her, when I scowled like her.

And I want to be angry with her, but it's like trying to be furious at a saint; I suppose to some people she is.

"We did not think you would be so young. We had hoped our work would find people old enough to bear this. But the magic is so ancient . . . Perhaps something went wrong."

"Do you think the other calonnau will be kids too?"

"I think it's quite likely, yes, given you and Dara are the same age, no?"

"We're in the same school too."

"Goodness," she whispers. "We always did feel a pull to each other. I suppose that has not changed."

We let silence fill the space again. The water ripples occasionally, like fish swim beneath the surface.

"I don't have any choice in this, do I?" I whisper.

She holds her hand out to me, palm up, and I take it. Her skin is so very cold.

"If I don't help Dara and Gelert find the others . . . If I don't help fight, then something bad is going to happen, isn't it?"

Nimuë doesn't need to answer because we both

know that I'm right, but she squeezes my hand anyway.

"You must trust your Ceridwen. Dara," she says, eventually.

"I know they are a good person, but . . ."

"Trusting people feels impossible?"

I nod. She gets it, and I wonder what happened to her to make her feel this way.

"Let Dara show you their heart. Ceridwen was a brilliant, clever person. Your Dara will be too. And they will need you."

I don't want to accept my fate. But, maybe the reason I forgot to tell Dara and Gelert this yesterday is because some part of me already has. I don't really understand who Arawn is, or what he wants yet, but it involves me. I can't ignore it. In a way, it's all I've ever wanted. All those stories and adventures with Mumma were me longing for something meaningful, that could be mine.

I just wish it didn't come with so many new people and potential mortal peril. I'm still not sure which is worse.

"Vivi, if you had not already accepted your role in the fight, we would not have been able to speak," Nimuë says, as if she read my mind. "Remember, dear child, I know exactly how stubborn we both can be."

We share a smile, as the world starts to leach of colour.

"You are waking up. We will speak again," she says, helping me to my feet.

The tiny patch of land I stand on drifts away from her, through an empty void. I can still hear her words echoing in my head as I wake up covered in cool sweat, with Excalibur in my hand.

Chapter Ten

It's barely a surprise to find Dara at my kitchen table the next morning.

"Oh, here she is," beams Mumma, as I pad in. She plants a kiss on my nest of hair. "I made pancakes!"

"Morning Vee!" says Dara with a cheerfulness that has no place anywhere near me at eight am on a Saturday.

"Hi," I yawn.

Apparently talking to Nimuë means I didn't sleep well, like when you have a really vivid dream.

I take my usual seat, and Mumma sets a stack of pancakes in front of me. A blueberry rolls off and plinks off the floor.

"If only we had a dog," laughs Mumma, retrieving it, and I wonder if Gelert eats table scraps.

"Look at this, peanut. Dara made this jacket!" Mam has threatened many times that the next hobby she's going to 'seriously get into' is making clothes, so she is naturally thrilled about this.

A pink blush spreads across their cheeks. "Oh, it's nothing really. Just practice and good patterns."

The jacket really is very beautiful, and nothing like I've seen anyone our age wear before. The fabric is thick and soft, patterned in black and gold. The threads glitter in the morning light. Mam makes them hold it open so I can appreciate the deep red lining. It is amazing that they made it; it looks straight out of a posh shop.

"Sorry, I should have checked if you were an early riser yesterday."

I shrug, shovelling pancakes into my mouth.

"If it would be alright with you both," Dara says in their most sweet parent-pleasing voice, "I'd like to show Vivi the big park on the hill. There are these really cool, old dinosaur statues that are kind of famous."

My ears prick up at the word dinosaurs, my first special interest. When I was little, I memorised a gigantic dinosaur book. It feels so good to just focus on something I love. Though sometimes I'd prefer to just turn my brain off and sleep than look up more facts.

"Yeah, can I?" I ask.

The Mums shoot excited glances at each other, that I know I'm not supposed to see but do anyway.

"Of course, honey. I was thinking we'd go check out the pool down the road, but we can do that tomorrow?"

A new pool. On one hand, great – I need to swim. I can feel my brain getting backed up from not floating around or doing laps. But also, public pools mean chlorine and people. What I liked about the lake was that no one else was there.

"There's actually one up there that I can show you too?" offers Dara.

I bob my head in response.

"How kind of you sweetie." Mumma squeezes Dara's shoulders like they're old friends, not two people who met only twelve hours ago.

Mumma drives us to the park. We hop out at the top of the steepest hill in the world, and she promises to meet us at the bottom of the park in two hours.

It's a bright, clear September day; warm sun and chilly air. It's not as cold as Wales, but I've underdressed in my puffy armless gilet. I rub at goose-bumps under my shirt sleeves. Luckily, my legs are warm in my old thermal tights and boots.

"Are you okay?" they ask, as we walk towards a large plasterboard map of the park.

Truthfully, I'm nervous about going somewhere new with someone I barely know but I feel too embarrassed to say that. I run the tip of my plait through my fingers, back and forth, until the wriggling in my stomach starts to dull. "I didn't sleep well. I spoke to Nimuë."

"No way!" they yell excitedly. "That's so cool that you got to talk to her. What's she like?"

"Floaty, but nice," I say, squinting at the map.

The park is shaped like a shield. "We're up here, and I'm going to lead you all the way through here, and eventually we will end up here." They trace their finger along the route so I can see. "If you want to go home early, we can just call your Mums."

"I know," I say frowning. Obviously, I can call my Mums.

"Well, yeah, but I mean you don't have to feel weird about doing it. I won't take it personally. You've had a big week."

"Oh, sorry," I say, my cheeks burning furiously as I realise they're being considerate. Truthfully, I'm not used to it. People used to be weird when I needed to go home in the middle of a sleepover or a party, and eventually the invites stopped coming.

"Unless you're actually fed up of me," they smile.

"Quite possible," I say, and we laugh – it feels like some of the awkwardness has lifted.

They lead me through a planted garden, where the last few flowers bloom, overlooked by an armless statue. The path opens up to a grand staircase and a plateau of bright green grass. We're so high up that the rest of South London stretches out below us.

I think of home, and my new home. Tower blocks crowd the skyline in place of mountains, and from where I stand on the steps, the sky feels almost as wide. It's greener than I expected here – trees and parks and little woods. There's no salt spray in the air, but it's still kind of beautiful.

"I've always wanted to show someone this view for the first time," Dara smiles as I gawp.

We continue on, through people in exercise gear stretching muscles and bumping bike tires.

"I know it looks busy but stick with me. It's a

triathlon day," explains Dara. "Running, swimming, and cycling. It all takes place up here and in the sports centre. And because this part of the park is gets busy on race days, the rest is usually empty. Hopefully it'll just be us and the dinos."

"You really thought of everything."

Dara flashes a grin at me. "I'm not just a pretty face, Vee."

We hurry past the lycra-clad people and their gigantic water bottles, and down some steps into the rest of the park. It's only then that I realise Gelert is with us.

"You didn't jump this time," he says. "Nice work."

I scowl at him. He's right, I do scowl.

"Gelert, you could be living the life playing ball and getting your belly scratched if you weren't so keen to be smug and annoying," I huff.

Dara bursts into laughter.

Gelert shakes his haunches. His wiry fur glitters silver in the sunlight. "I'm not smug, mun."

"Smuggest dog I've ever met,' chimes in Dara.

He huffs and stalks off ahead.

It's quiet away from the racers and Dara was right: this bit is almost empty. We walk down a tree-lined avenue where the leaves are already turning copper. Gelert leads us past large ponds, filled with birds. Ducks boldly saunter across paths, not remotely bothered by Gelert or us. Perhaps they know he's a ghost so can't eat them.

And then I see the dinosaurs. Or, what people used to think dinosaurs looked like, a long time ago. They have a greenish tinge to them and are a little worse for wear.

Dara leads me up a slope to a bench that overlooks them, and we sit. I scuff my boots in the dust as I take them all in.

"I love them," I say.

"Me too."

"Thanks for bringing me here."

I can't stop looking at the big statues. They're impressive, even if they're also a bit inaccurate and maybe even a bit weird-looking in places where they've worn away.

"You're welcome."

A little further down the slope, Gelert lies down in a patch of clover.

"Do you . . ." I begin.

"Do I what?"

I want to ask them whether this frightens them. Whether they lie in bed at night and wonder why they have to be a chosen one.

"Do you think it's safe to practice?" I find myself asking instead.

"We don't have to do anything today if you don't want to," they say, giving me a look.

"I know."

From my backpack, I take a bottle of water and set it on the bench between us. It's warm out, so I take a sip and pocket the cap. Dara refuses a sip, and I'm not sure if it's out of politeness or if they're worried about drinking all my ammo.

"Let's do a warm-up," they say. "We know you've mastered stirring and almost exploding it over our classmates, but practice makes perfect."

Their palm faces the sky, and from seemingly nowhere, purple sparks run along their skin. They must pull electricity right out of the world.

"Every time you use your powers, you understand them better, and know how it should feel."

In one deep breath out, the sparks disappear completely.

"Your turn," they say.

The whirlpool comes easily.

"Can you manipulate its shape? Like, what about a water rope like the afanc used."

My stomach fizzes at the name, but I try to concentrate. I haven't tried anything like this since that last morning in our old bathroom, or rather, I haven't done it intentionally.

Gelert appears at my knee. "Relax. You're not trying to terrify the water into obeying, eh. Stop scowling at it."

"I'm not scowling."

"You blinking well are. You're doing it now."

"Just a little," added Dara.

I shake my head and try to rearrange my face into an expression that conveys I'm both relaxed and concentrating. "Better?"

"Worse," says the dog.

I puff out my cheeks in frustration.

Purposefully trying to use my powers is hard. Now that I'm trying, nothing is happening.

"Relax."

"You know what's not relaxing?" I hiss, not taking my eyes from the bottle. "Being told to relax."

I think back to my sessions with Dr May. When

things went bad, we worked on ways to calm myself down. Closed eyes, deep breaths, and clench one muscle group at a time − toes, calves, thighs, all the way up body.

And I think of the still water. How we could be the same.

Dara stifles a gasp. I open one eye. A thin rope of water stands upright out of the bottle.

Higher, I think, and it rises, thin and straight as a crystal shard.

"Look who it is," says a familiar voice.

My attention breaks and water explodes all over me. The bottle falls off the bench, rolling down the slope.

On the path below us are Chia and Stevie, whose foot rests on the bottle.

Chapter Eleven

"Hey guys!" cries Chia. She picks up the bottle from under Stevie's foot and skips up the hill towards us. The skirt of her pink dress puffs up and down like a jellyfish.

Stevie follows, slinking towards us like a panther in her shiny black and red exercise clothes.

"Funny seeing you here!" says Dara a little too loudly.

"Did they see?" I whisper.

"I don't know!" They're panicking, which unnerves me more than Stevie's glare.

"I love it here," says Chia, reaching us and perching on the dry bench arm next to Dara. "Mummy always used to bring Ife and me to feed peas to the ducks. Once we saw a rat eating a samosa. It was great! Is this your first time seeing the dinosaurs Vivi?"

Chia appears to be the sort of person who is just incredibly pleased by everything happening to them at all times. She holds out my dirty water bottle, and I wipe some of the muck off against my dark tights.

"Yeah, Dara wanted to show me them. They're . . . interesting."

Chia laughs. "That's for sure. Have you seen that one's face?" She points to a long low dinosaur crouching in the mud. Its mouth lolls open and I can't help but laugh when she does an alarmingly good impression of it. "I'm rubbish at art, but even I can draw a dinosaur better than that."

"To be fair, they were made before anyone knew what a dinosaur really looked like," says Dara. "Plus, there's other animals hidden in the trees. We can go find them all in a bit."

"I didn't think this would be your thing, Dar," sniffs Stevie, scuffing the ground with a shiny looking sneaker.

"Dinosaurs?" asks Chia.

"Statues?" I ask.

"Being outside," she answers.

"I go outside. Look at me, I'm outside right now!" they protest. Their ears go bright pink. It's the first time I've seen Dara look awkward, like their skin fits wrong

"Okay, but you're wearing suede shoes and a blazer to sit by a duck pond."

"There's nothing wrong with looking nice."

"And they made that jacket themselves," I say, taken over by a sudden urge to defend Dara.

"Obviously," Stevie replies bluntly. "Not likely to find something like that on the high street."

"Is there a compliment hidden underneath all that?" Chia says, as she playfully elbows Stevie in the ribs.

"Yes, you look nice," Stevie mutters, as she smooths down the mesh of her running top.

The blush on Dara's ears spreads across their cheeks.

"Was that so hard?" Chia teases.

"Yes," she says, before turning her attention to me. "Why is it whenever we meet, you're throwing bottles of water around?"

"Everyone needs a hobby," I laugh, a little too loud.

Now that she mentions it, I am soaked. My gilet has absorbed so much water, I feel like I'm wearing a sponge.

"We're not all as coordinated as you," Dara says softly.

"I have one hand and I'm less clumsy than both of you combined," she says, a smile breaking through at the corners of her mouth.

The atmosphere changes. Dara and Stevie bicker, but there's something else underneath it all. Maybe a kind of history? At first, I thought Stevie was just immune to Dara's charm, but it's not quite that either. I can't work it out.

"Are you racing today?" Dara asks.

"Is that not obvious?" Stevie says, gesturing at her outfit. "Yes. Chia was helping me warm up."

"I'm really good at yelling out all the different stretches she has to do," Chia says proudly.

"Yeah, because you've got a loud gob."

"It's called vocal projection, Stevie Lim. But yes, I do." She's so proud of herself that we can't help but laugh with her.

"Don't let us keep you," I say. "You don't want to cool down too much."

Stevie arches an eyebrow. "Do you race?"

"Oh, no. No. I just used to swim a lot. In a lake."

Stevie scrunches up her nose. "In a lake? Like, full of weeds and fish?"

Before I can try to explain why swimming in a lake

110

is actually fine, I realise that Chia is petting Gelert. "Hey, whose dog is this anyway?"

"My . . . neighbour's!" answers Dara, the flush on their cheeks now fully red. "You know what it's like with big dogs, never get enough exercise, ha ha, so we decided we'd bring him out to the park for a good walk, and it turns out he really likes the dinosaurs."

"He's a very good boy. A very, *very* good boy," coos Chia. "What's his name?"

"Gelert," we say, and at his name the dog looks over, embarrassed that his tail was wagging so hard that his bottom was wagging too.

"I need to head up to the race," says Stevie, checking the watch on her wrist. "You should dry off or you'll catch a chill, Vivi."

"Okay, let's go." Chia hops off the bench and pats Gelert three times on his forehead. "Bye bye friends!"

Once they're out of sight, we all let go of a long breath.

"What was that?" I ask.

"What was what?"

"You. The blabbering and the blushing."

"Oh," they look down at their feet. "She makes me nervous, you know? I always feel like a dork when she's around."

"Welcome to my life with basically everyone," I say, flopping back against the bench.

"Well, it's not quite like—"

"And you!" I hiss, turning to Gelert. "Could you not have hidden?"

But he doesn't answer.

He's staring intently at the dinosaurs. The hair that runs down his spine rises in a thick hairy ridge, and a very deep growl pours out of his throat.

"What is it?" Dara asks, and we both peer into the distance.

Crouched between the legs of the goofy crocodile-like dinosaur is something strange. The creature, definitely not an animal I've ever seen before, runs from one statue to another. It scuttles on all fours with legs that stick out straight from its body like an insect's. It is the deepest, pitch dark black all over. The edges of its body move like pencil scribbles, like it's here but only just.

"Nothing good," growls Gelert.

Over the sound of the birds, I hear a metallic rattling noise. It sounds like it's coming through a speaker, but somehow, I know it's from that creature.

Suddenly it shoots off, diving headfirst into one of the ponds.

"Quickly," says Gelert, setting off after it.

We race over a wooden bridge and run down a path that circles the edge of the lake. Panicked birds swarm in the air, and I have to duck to avoid a pigeon going full pelt towards my head.

As we run, I hear the whistle that starts the triathlon cut through the air, followed by cheers.

Before we can catch up, the creature rushes out of the water, across the path, and up the side of the coffee shop. It climbs the walls with ease, on all fours like a lizard. Perched on the roof, it looks around, surveying the park.

Dara and I keep low, crouching behind a statue of a gorilla that is, for some reason, here.

Gelert stalks through the bushes around the lake behind us. I glance back, and see his fur fading, like he's half trying to disappear and half trying really hard to stay.

"What is it Gel?" asks Dara.

Gelert shushes them with a growl. But the creature has already heard.

Its head turns too far around on its neck, one

hundred and eighty degrees.

Now we're closer, I can see it much clearer. The two large circles on the side of its head uncurl like a butterfly tongue, stretching out to very large, pointed ears.

Where eyes should be are four bright red burning circles, pointed straight towards us.

I can't tell if it sees us.

I hope not.

Mumma told me so many stories about monsters, but unlike the afanc, I have no idea what this pitch-black fuzzy insect monster is. It moves like smoke, barely there.

Beside me, Dara trembles. I steady them with a hand, and they relax against me.

The monster's head snaps away from us, and, in a blink, it leaps into the nearest tree. It bounds from tree to tree down the main avenue of the park. Right towards the triathlon.

We scrabble to our feet, following as quickly and quietly as we can.

The cheers and whistles of the triathlon grow louder, mixed with honking bike horns and tinkling bells. The chorus of voices swim in my head. I'm still clutching onto Dara, luckily.

"Where did it go?" Dara hisses, pulling me behind a tree.

Gelert crouches behind us, low to the ground.

"There!" he whispers, pointing his nose towards a small playground just ahead of us.

Where Chia sits on a swing, looking at something in her hand while idly swaying back and forth. Her patent sandals scuff in the dust.

"Oh no," whispers Dara.

Just above her, standing on the top of the swings, is the creature. It's legs crowd over the frame, like a spider in the corner of a room.

Everything about this feels wrong.

Chia is in danger.

There's no time to think of a plan.

I run straight for Chia.

"Chia!" I yell, with all the breath in my lungs.

If I can get to her first, then maybe she will be okay.

The last thing I see is her happy face as the monster jumps down.

And they both disappear in a cloud of grey.

Chapter Twelve

Dara and I collide into the little fence around the playground, both staring at the space where Chia was, only moments ago.

"Where did she go?!" I gasp.

She's gone.

She's just . . . gone.

After a moment, Dara quietly walks into the playground and drops to their knees in front of the swing.

"There's nothing here," Dara whispers, their voice thick with tears.

"I don't understand what happened. Did it grab her? They just vanished!" I blabber.

"Hopefully, it just took her," Gelert says. He walks into the playground while sniffing the air and the ground, ignoring the No Dogs sign on the gate.

I can't move, not yet. My knuckles are white with how hard I'm gripping the fence.

"What was that *thing* Gelert?" I whisper.

"I'm not sure yet," he says. "But I think I know where it came from."

He walks up to the swing and starts taking very deep huffs. I brave the playground and stand next to Dara, who is shaking slightly. It freaks me out to see them so afraid; I thought they were the strong one in this pairing.

Eventually Gelert looks up. "Aether," he says, an answer to a question we didn't ask yet.

"What is aether?" Dara asks, their voice vibrating as much as their body.

"Matter, or a kind of matter. What things are made of."

"So, a molecule or an atom?" they continue.

"Close enough. Or rather, it's the gaps between. It's where they sit, and how those molecules move, or change."

This all goes over my head. I really am not very science-y, despite my love for space and the planets. I just know a lot of facts and like to imagine stories around them. This is testing my very limited understanding.

Gelert must spot that I'm not remotely following. "I can 'teleport', right?"

"Right," I nod.

"But I'm not actually teleporting. I'm making holes, or portals, by manipulating aether."

"But holes to where?"

He draws two lines in the dirt. "Remember I told you there's our world, and there's the Kingdoms of Other?"

I nod, and he draws another wiggly line between the two.

"In the middle, is the Unlands. It's not really a place in the same way your town has places to live and eat and go do things. It's more like a place to travel through."

"So, like a corridor?"

"Aye, close enough. Usually, I'm going within the seams of our world."

Dara looks at the watch on their wrist and nudges me. "Vivi it's time to go."

"Yes, you should get out of here, just in case," Gelert says, and returns to his sniffing.

We start to walk towards the car park, but a cold

dread fills my stomach. "Wait, do you think those monsters are connected to . . . the rest of this?"

I don't have to say any more because Dara knows what I mean. The spell. The trapped King. The magic in our fingers.

"I'm worried it could be," whispers Dara.

No wonder Gelert sent us away. I twist the end of my plait around my fingers. "What should we do?"

"What do you mean?"

"Like, do we go to the police?"

"And tell them what? If we told them we saw a monster snatch a girl in front of us, we'd be laughed out the police station."

They're right. I know they're right.

"Oh God, Stevie," they whisper. "Stevie's going to finish her race and then realise Chia's not there. And then she's going to find out Chia is missing."

"And we can't tell her either," I whisper. "But we have to find her. Somehow."

We say nothing else as we walk to the car park. Mumma stands leaning against the car and waves her arms as she sees us approach.

"Let's act normal, or we'll freak your Mum out," Dara whispers, mimicking her wave.

119

I nod, and both of us plaster on fake smiles and hope for the best.

Mumma seems not to notice that we're faking it, and chats away happily about the shops in Crystal Palace that she walked around. The boot is full of plants from the little garden centre.

We drop Dara off, and when we get inside, I say I need to go lie down to de-stimulate my brain. The Mums send me up with a slice of cake, happy that I've been out making friends.

But I've also just lost one.

Literally, lost.

I lie down on the bed and burst into tears.

What if she's hurt? What if she's *scared*? Chia is so nice and good and practically the only person I've felt I can trust properly and now she's just gone. And I can't help but feel like it's all my fault for not stopping it. What's the good of this magic if I can't help people?

I had just about accepted the fact that I wasn't going to be able to escape from this whole magical destiny thing – I mean you don't have a magical dream-vision where you speak to your soul through the medium of an ancient sword without thinking it's not optional.

But now, I'm so angry.

What was that thing? And what does it want with Chia?

My eyes drift to my bookshelf. When we started our adventures around Wales, Mumma gave me a huge book of Welsh myths. I read it so much that the spine had to be taped up.

I slide off the bed, slide it gently from the shelves and open it in my lap.

Those creatures must be in here.

Over the next few hours, I read through the stories. I used to know them off by heart, but I'd forgotten a bunch. Of course, the first one is the afanc terrorising a small town by flooding it. I don't think I'll ever forget any of their stories after meeting one. I keep going, past the sunken city under the sea, the warring dragons, the girl made of flowers.

A storm rises outside, wind battering the trees. But there's nothing in my book that looks like that monster. I close it, frustrated.

I could try Google, but I feel like searching for *horrible possibly spider thing that steals children* might bring up some real nightmare fuel. And that's when I remember that strange blog. Shadows . . . someone asked something about shadows.

Before I can find my tablet, Gelert appears.

"Did you find anything?" I ask, my chest bursting with hope.

He hangs his head, and I feel the heartbreak all over again.

"Gelert, do you think it was looking for me and Dara? Like, it can't be a coincidence that this monster just showed up where we were, right? I'd never seen a monster before I got the sword, and now I've seen two. Plus you."

"Luckily, I'm not a monster," he sniffs, lying down on the rug next to me. "I've not ruled it out."

"That you're a monster?"

"That this is Arawn's doing. He's likely still bound by the magic, at the very least stuck in Annwn, else we'd certainly have heard from him."

"You've told me bits about him, but like, what does he actually want?"

"Arawn wanted to . . . or wants to . . . conquer the human world. He lived here for a time, disguised as a true King. Got a taste for it, like. But he's greedy. He doesn't just want your human world. He wants both yours and Annwn."

"How would that work? Hopefully he can't be in two places at once?"

"Not as far as I know," Gelert says, which doesn't fill me with confidence. "He wants to bridge the gap between the worlds, take down the aether barrier."

"That sounds . . . bad," I say.

"Given that the Other is full of monsters desperate to come wreak havoc in your world, I'd say so."

"Monsters that he can get onside," I murmur.

"Possibly. He's a smart man and a nasty sort, but he's clever about it. Knows how to spin a story and to give people just enough of what they want so they stay loyal to him."

He sounds exhausted, at least as tired as I am. I can't imagine carrying this story, these secrets, for a thousand years alone, just waiting to have to break the news to someone.

"What does he even want with our world?"

"Oh, what do these dictator-Kings ever want," he scoffs. "Bodies, fealty, power. It's all the same. And if he can't get it, a bloody war between the worlds will entertain him well enough. He's a threat to you all, and he'll destroy your world as you know it. Chia is just the start."

"What if we can't get her back Gel," I whisper. "What if we're not strong enough?"

"You are," he murmurs. "You have to be."

He rests his body against me, and I go back to the book, paying attention to every word, just in case I might miss a clue.

"What's that then?" he mutters in his sleep.

"A book of the old stories."

"Am I in it?" he asks, one eye open.

"Nothing about annoying ghost dogs in the index," I say, pretending to look.

He huffs at me, and I'm actually glad I'm not alone right now. I should go and see Dara tomorrow, so we can talk this all through.

Gelert's right. We have to be strong, and we have to find Chia.

Chapter Thirteen

The next morning, I walk over to Dara's house. Mam had rung ahead to make sure that they were in and that it was okay for me to come over on a Sunday, and Mr. McLeod, Dara's father, had apparently tried to invite everyone over. I insisted I go alone this time, and the Mums agreed, proud of me for going somewhere new alone.

Going to someone's house for the first time always makes me nervous. Everyone has their own rules, and they don't always tell you what they are because they think they're the same for everyone. Except everyone has totally different 'normals'.

Their house is part of a terrace row like mine but painted bright white, with red brick roofs and tall chimney stacks. The front door is deep blue and has a big bronze knocker in the middle of it. I lift it and try to gently knock, but it's more like a bang.

The door flings open.

"Welcome to our humble abode!"

Dara is dressed in a bright jade green suit jacket over a bright golden shirt, with a small red velvet bowtie. I'm now realising that this is how Dara dresses all the time. Even at home.

I suddenly feel underdressed in my scraggly knitted jumper and corduroy skirt.

"Hi," I say, as Dara shuts the door behind me. I add my stomping boots to a shoe rack overrun by very large but very, very white trainers; they must belong to their older brother, Rabbie.

"Let's go up to my room so we can talk a minute," they say quietly, leading me up the stairs.

"Are you dressed as a butler?" At the top of the stairs stands a boy younger than us, whose eyes are fixed on his Nintendo Switch. Like Dara, he has deep red hair, but it's shaved short against his skin. "Fetch me a snack! And a drink. Sweep the floor."

"No, I'm just very well-dressed Lachie!!" Dara pouts as we reach the landing. As he walks downstairs, Dara shouts after him. "Don't forget our deal!"

"Yeah yeah," he mutters, out of view.

"Sorry about my little brother," they say, pushing open the door to their surprisingly tidy bedroom. "He is the worst."

"I heard that!" Lachie yells from several rooms away.

On their desk sits a green lined cutting board illuminated by a large lamp. The set of drawers next to it is near-bursting with fabric, bits of cardboard, and even those wiggly neon pipe cleaners. We sit down on the bed next to each other, and I feel the pretence of downstairs lift.

"How are you feeling?" I ask.

"Not great," they say honestly. "You?"

"Same. There's just . . . so much going on."

"Yeah," they say.

"How do you stop it from getting to you?"

They sigh deeply. "Ask me that when it stops getting to me. There's so much I don't know, and what, because I woke up first, I'm supposed to be in charge of finding everyone else?"

I feel guilty that I hadn't thought about that before. So much has been placed on Dara's head.

"I'm just going along with this as much as I can, while trying not to blow up any more lightbulbs," they laugh. "Or being disappeared by some weird monster."

"Speaking of," I say, taking my tablet out of my bag. "I went through my myth books last night and didn't find anything, and Gelert had no idea what they were either. But I might have a lead."

"Strange Britain: we see what the normies do not," Dara says, reading from the website. "What is this?"

"On Friday night, after you'd been round and when I was kind of all over the place, I ended up googling like *is magic real*, you know?"

Dara nods sagely. "Who among us has not turned to Google to ask weird questions in our time of need."

"This is what came up. And there was this post about seeing shadows and it being evidence of magic," I say, scrolling down to it. "What if it's about the same monster?"

"Aha!" I say, clicking the 'read more' option at the bottom so we can see the whole thing.

To all my darling ghosts, ghouls and non-boonary pals, one of you lovely sprites tipped me off about a major sighting last week, which might also be linked to the disappearance of a child in South London.

The blog post includes an excerpt of an article from *The London Times*.

Clare Woodfine, 12, disappeared during a family trip to Streatham Common on the 1st of September. Family reported no unusual sightings, but that Clare disappeared within moments. Local police are appealing for any witnesses.

"That's only a week ago!" gasps Dara.

"I'd just moved here . . . Where's Streatham Common?"

"Just down the road."

"That makes three monsters near us," I whisper.

"Technically about 23 if you count all those coblyns."

"But you see what I mean? They all keep appearing near us."

Dara shudders and continues reading.

You might remember that on the same day, our dear friend **hexy666** wrote an impassioned piece collating reports of mysterious shadows. Thanks hexy for visiting the scarier parts of the internet so that we don't have to.

In summary, there have been multiple sightings of strange shadow creatures throughout South London. According to most of the local neighbourhood Facebook groups (the shadowiest part of the internet, if I may say so!) most of the normies believe the beast to be a particular large dog or a melanic and very angry fox (aka, black fur). However, as you'll see from the information hexy has collected, these don't tally up. No dogs leap about in trees, and the descriptions are much more arachnid.

Arachnid. Spider. I glance through the original post which has been quoted. Weird moving shadow bodies. Red circles. Quick movements in a blink of an eye. It must be the same monster.

And a lot of them. Or one very active monster.

And so, dear readers, I'm appealing to you. Have you seen one of these? Do you have any clue what they might be because, and I hate to admit this, I'm a little confounded. So, let us pool our resources and solve the mystery together, shall we.

Kiss kiss,

The Ghost Queen

"We should write in!" cries Dara. "Tell them what we saw."

"Really? Do you think that's a good idea?"

"Look, these people already know about it, so it's not like we're blowing our cover or anything. Maybe they can help us work out what it is? And where it's taken Chia."

"Like anonymous internet research assistants?"

"Exactly. It could end up being useless, but you never know. We're out of leads as it is."

They're right.

Mam says never read the comments, but I open them up anyway, just in case. Mostly it's people suggesting ways she could've disappeared, usually along the lines of vengeful ghosts or "it's obviously vampires".

"I'm not sure many of these people really know what they're talking about," I say, pulling up the neck of my t-shirt over my chin so I can concentrate better.

But then one comment catches my eye.

don'ttouchmykelpie *commented:*

I was there and the police won't listen to me. They've written me off as making things up for

131

**attention, but I know what I saw. She was walking
just behind her family, and then this dark black
creature with massive, long legs leapt out and they
disappeared in a cloud of smoke.**

A shiver runs down my spine. This is exactly what
happened to Chia.

"Oh no," whispers Dara. "So, they've definitely
taken another kid."

The realisation that they are possibly after us
hangs over our heads.

"I wonder how they're picking people though. Do
you think they're tracking our talismans? Or can they
sense magic, even if the calon's magic hasn't woken
up yet? Could they have found a way to hunt down
the others we haven't found yet?" They're just
offering up different theories, but my stomach
spins at every new and horrible idea.

"I don't know. I thought they were just trailing us,
but neither of us were in Streatham then, right?"

Dara shakes their head.

I click the new comment box, and start writing,
in a voice that sounds like I could be an adult
who comments here regularly. It takes me a few goes

to make it sound right.

Nimuë&ceridwen commented:

Dear Ghost Queen,

We are first time visitors to your site but wanted to tell you that we saw the same thing as **don'ttouchmykelpie**. These shadow-spider-monsters are real and took a young girl from Crystal Palace Park yesterday.

In addition to the other commenter's descriptions, we've observed them climbing walls like reptiles, leaping through trees and swimming through water. We hope this additional information will help you find out the identity of this creature.

"Using our calon's names isn't very subtle," says Dara, only once I've hit post this comment.

"It's got to be something witchy to convince them that we're one of them."

"Good point. Well, now that's done, I should show you what I was up to last night when I couldn't sleep."

They get to their feet, and, when I don't follow, pull me up off the bed.

"What's that then?" I ask.

"Weapons."

"Sorry?"

"Yeah, like. I know you've got a sword and technically I could take out an eye with my awl, but maybe we need some traps? Or something like that. Backups for the magic."

"You're right. What am I gonna do right now, stir them to death?"

"Mix them a really good drink."

"Bubble up their bubble bath."

We share a giggle, and everything feels easy. Scary, but easy.

"You'll get there. It takes practice and time."

"Which we might not have if they show up again. Do you have something in mind? This weapon situation, I mean"

"Oh boy, do I."

Chapter Fourteen

I wasn't quite prepared for Dara to say they'd been researching weapons, but before I can respond they usher me downstairs to the kitchen at the back of the house. It's a big, bright room, with copper pans hanging on the wall, and a whole row of cookbooks. There's a lot of baking cookbooks.

A tall, broad-shouldered man weighs out flour into a big mixing bowl. Built like a rugby player, as Mam would say.

"Pops, Vivi's here."

Any nerves I had disappear under his warm smile; it reminds me so much of Dara's.

"Lovely to meet you Vivi. Welcome to our house," he says. His Scottish accent is very, very thick.

"Hello Mr. McLeod," I say.

"Bruce is fine, Vivi. No need for formalities." He pauses to give Dara a stern look. "Dara McLeod, don't you even think about taking that jacket into the garden. If it gets messy while you're playing with your wee gadgets, I'll not be the one to clean it."

Dara sighs. "Okayyyy."

They go to hang it on the back of a chair at the dining table, but Bruce, without looking up, coughs pointedly.

"Fine, I'll go hang it up."

They dash off upstairs, leaving Bruce and I alone in the kitchen.

"Dara gets a little over excited about their inventions – they get that from me. The play too, I suppose."

"I'm the same about space, and nature . . . and a lot of things I guess," I say shyly.

He laughs warmly. "I think they're happy to have someone to share it with."

If only he knew.

"What are you making?" I ask, hoping it doesn't sound nosey.

"I'm trying out a new Sacher Torte recipe. Have you eaten one?"

I shake my head. "What is it?"

"It's a really, really rich chocolate cake, with apricot jam in there too. I know it sounds a bit of a silly mix, but it works!" he laughs.

"Do you bake a lot?"

"Oh aye, I find it relaxing. Baking takes a lot of patience. Take this Sacher Torte – the recipe says it's better if you let it sit for a day."

"Wow. I'm not very good at being patient."

"Me either, but this is a good way to practice," he says, with a wink.

Dara returns, now wearing a purple and yellow patterned fleecy jumper.

"Ah, the brilliant inventor returns!" Bruce says.

"Thank you for recognising my talents," they say with a swish.

From by the back door, Dara passes me a pair of superhero patterned gardening clogs, which are a little too small for me but I make do.

"Good luck," calls Bruce, a cloud of flour rising in the air as he folds the open bag back down. "Don't get too cold. Or be too loud, Mum's studying remember."

The back garden is a big wide-open lawn bordered by flowerbeds, with a shed and an ancient looking

Wendy house at the end. A little black dog with curly fur and the biggest shiny black eyes trots out after us, carrying an orange ball in her mouth.

"No, Callie, it's not play time."

Resigned, the ball drops from Callie's mouth.

While Dara disappears into the Wendy house, I hold out my hand for Callie to sniff. She gives me a lick with her tiny pink tongue, so I scratch behind her ears.

"Step inside my office," Dara calls.

Even though I'm not particularly tall, I still have to duck my head to get into the Wendy house. Just to be safe, I close the door behind me to keep Callie away from whatever potentially explosive inventions Dara is about to share with me.

"Was this yours when you were a little kid?"

"It was," they say wistfully. "But now it's the perfect storage for my creations."

A big metal box sits between us on the floor. Dara undoes the clasp on the lid with a practiced flick.

"Now, I've been coming up with some solutions for our monster problem. We know we're probably going to see them again if they're popping up all over London, so we should be prepared."

My stomach churns at this.

"So, we know they're fast, can climb trees, can swim—"

"—And are horrible," I add.

"Very horrible. And if we are going to find out where they took Chia and the others, I think we need to catch one. Or at least, when we next see one, we can slow it down a bit."

"That might give us a chance to work out what it is or learn more about it," I say, shuddering at the thought of getting close to one.

In a flash, Gelert appears on the bench next to me. He's so big that he has to hunch over to fit into the tiny space. He looks ridiculous.

A giggle bursts out of both Dara and me.

"Ey. Stop your laughing," he huffs.

Realising another dog is in her garden, Callie starts a high-pitched and extremely angry *yip yip yip* right outside the door.

Dara pokes their head out of the tiny window. "Callie, go get Lachie!"

The little dog does a bouncy yap, clearly happy to have been acknowledged, as Dara withdraws their head and closes the shutter.

"What are you going to do if you catch one, eh?

Have a little chat over some bara brith, is it? We don't even know if they can speak, mun," snorts Gelert.

"Hmm, and it might do that disappeary-cloud-of-smoke thing even if we did," I add.

"Can you both stop being such giant negs and let me tell you the rest of my plan?"

From the box they pull out a long cardboard tube, and a net.

"It's just a prototype," they say, taking it out of the Wendy house. I follow, but Gelert stays behind, peeking his head out of the window.

They extend it to be longer, like you might do with a telescope, and at the end they attach the net which sticks out like a folded-up umbrella.

"Who stole my clogs?" Lachie stumbles into the garden in a pair of too-big gardening shoes.

"Oh. Sorry," I say, wiggling my foot.

He gives me a grunt which I presume means I can keep wearing them for now.

"Alright, let's do this. And then you're doing all my chores for a week, remember Dar?"

"I said four days, Lachie!"

He crosses his arms. "Well, I'm the one about to get shot so I think it's only fair."

"I'm sorry, did you say shot?" I interrupt but I'm ignored by both McLeods.

"Alright, alright. Stand over there, would you?" Dara grumbles. "Little brothers, I tell you."

As instructed, Lachie stands in the middle of the lawn, arms by his sides.

"Ready?"

"Ready." He gives us a thumbs-up.

Dara raises their invention, aims, and shoots.

The knitted net flies through the air and . . .

Lands on Lachie's head.

It just about reaches his neck. With one shrug, the net slides off his head and falls to the floor, where Callie sniffs it dubiously.

"Erm, *wow*," I say, genuinely trying to sound enthusiastic, but I'm worried in my confusion it comes out sarcastic.

"Bit rubbish, isn't it? I didn't even need to try to escape," says Lachie, picking up the net and throwing it over to Dara. "Plus, it's tiny."

"It's just a scale prototype," Dara says, as though this was obvious. "The real one will be bigger. This is to test if the idea works."

Net reattached, I take the machine from Dara.

It's very light, all cardboard except for a couple of plastic tubes at the top. The net is made out of thick gardening twine and is woven into knots, like the ones I used to see hanging from fishing boats in the harbour. It's actually way more complicated than it looked when they first got it out.

"I can't believe you made this. *How* did you make this?"

"These plunger tubes from syringes are activated by this switch, which is attached to these wires," they say, pointing out all the components. "I think the net needs more weight, or maybe some more propulsion."

"Where did you even get all this stuff?"

They distractedly point at the shed. "Pops' two hobbies are making things out of stuff he finds on the ground and practicing to be on *Great British Bake Off*."

It might not be enough to catch a monster right now, but it's the start of something, I'm sure of it.

"I'm impressed," I say.

"Just something I found online and rejigged a little for our purposes. Anyway, round two!"

Out from the Wendy house they bring out another cardboard tube, but this one is enormous and looks heavy. Sticking out from the end are plastic arrows.

"Err, Dara—" I begin as they point it right at Lachine.

"Ready!!!" they call, lining up the shot.

"Um!" whimpers Lachie.

At the pull of a lever, the barrel of the cardboard tube starts to spin. Faster and faster, until it suddenly begins shooting out the plastic arrows as it turns. These fly all over the garden, all but one missing Lachie. The one that landed is stuck to the middle of his forehead by the sucker end.

"Is that a gatling gun?" he shrieks, pulling the arrow from his head with a pop. "Nah man, I'm out. This is some villain business."

He drops it on the grass and stalks off back inside the house.

Dara shrugs as he leaves. "I haven't worked out how to scale this one up. It's pretty heavy. But I used fidget spinner insides to make it spin, cool huh!"

"Err Dara, I don't think we can exactly go around with a gun. People might notice."

"I was hoping Gel would carry it for us. Like, what if we strapped it to him?"

"Not a flipping chance!" he hisses from the window.

Hearing him, Callie starts barking loudly again.

"Oh well. Not every idea is the right one. Was fun to make."

"I'm a little scared to ask if there's anything else . . ." I say.

"Not right now. I've got some ideas, and I tried making some kind of sticky slime to catch them, but I keep just making normal slime. Hey, you want some slime?"

The net gun is still in my hands, so I aim it straight ahead at the shed, out of the way of any living targets. It's light, and the net flies much further than I expected it to.

With a few changes, maybe it will be something we can use. If not to catch them, it could still distract them, disarm them. Maybe it'll be just enough to give us an edge.

"I think this one is a winner."

They give me a huge smile. "That's the spirit!"

Chapter Fifteen

I'm in a dark blue cave and, if it weren't for all the talking and flickering screens and the other people, I could quite happily live here forever, I think.

The Science Museum is enormous. After I left Dara's yesterday, I lay in bed going through the maps and exhibition information, so I had some idea of what we would be doing today. What I didn't anticipate is just how big it is in here. Or how many people would be here.

I love going to museums, but they can be hard. Noise, flashing lights on displays, visitors. It all adds up. Mr. Reynolds said I could wear my headphones, but I decided not to for a bit, while I can.

The Science Club spreads out in the Atmosphere exhibition room, twos and threes huddling around displays. Almost all of us.

Chia isn't here obviously. When we were lined up at school, ready to go get on the train, I could feel her absence like a hole. Mr. Reynolds didn't say anything about it, and no one asked Stevie because she looked like a literal storm cloud. When Dara tried to speak to her, she practically ran off and has been keeping a solid distance from us at all times. She must know that Chia is missing, but doesn't want to talk about it, or maybe isn't allowed to. I can't imagine what she's feeling, but given we were there when she last saw Chia, we must be reminders of what's happening.

The deep exhausted heaviness I've been feeling for days pulls at me. I wish I could be benched for today, but part of me wants to keep going, even though my vision is slightly blurry. Mumma definitely noticed I was tired this morning, but I just made sure my mouth was full of toast every time she asked me if I was sure I didn't want to do a half day, or stay home, and made sure to rush around in order to look like I was excited for school. I've no idea if she bought it, but I'm here at least.

Beside me, Dara prods at an interactive screen

explaining climate change.

"Normal weather patterns . . ." they mutter.

"Not becoming a climate change denier, I hope?" But they don't look up.

On screen is a new page about extreme weather events in the UK. Rainstorms and flooding; heatwaves, and forest fires.

"Do you think people are chalking up the weird weather that happened when we woke up to climate change?" they say. "Wait, what if we're causing it?"

I'm not quite sure if they're being serious – I'm too tired – but I know climate anxiety is a big deal for a lot of people, so, to be safe, I pat them on the shoulder.

"I don't think our two weeks over the summer explains all this" I say, pointing to the displays about sea level rise, wildfires, and monsoons. "Although, if it had been kids with magic powers all along, we'd have an enormous army which might be helpful with the whole fighting monsters thing."

"True. Nice to have one thing to not feel extremely guilty about."

The pat was probably the right call.

"It was really hot that week. I hope no one got

sick, and that nothing set on fire," they add.

"That's not your fault though," I say, sensing that we might not be talking about weather, really.

"Mmhmm."

"I mean, unless you were *specifically* like hey universe make it searingly hot while I get my sparky powers."

They laugh at me. "Alright, I'll stop beating myself up this one time."

"Good."

I have probably spent more time with Dara in the last four days than I have with anyone other my parents for . . . years maybe. And in that time, I've started to notice a few things. In the same way I mask some of my autism traits, Dara's not always their full self with other people. They're a worrier. It creeps out in jokes, in small moments when they think people aren't paying attention.

But I do.

"I wonder what the next weird weather thing will be. Personally, I hope it's raining frogs," they say, pulling me over to a display about animals involved in weather events.

"Tadpoles, fish and frogs fell in a storm in Japan," I read out.

"We can skip the fish," they say, sticking their tongue out. "But frogs though? I really like frogs."

"Do you have a favourite species of frog?" I ask, biting on my tongue as soon as I finish. This is the sort of question that Kelly Keane used to tell me was for babies, and not what cool people talked about. I'm never quite sure if those rules were actually real but hot shame still runs through my blood.

But to my relief, Dara spins round and yells, "THE COSTA RICAN BLUE JEAN DART FROG IS MY FAVOURITE!"

They pull up their phone to show me their lock screen. A bright red frog with blue legs sits on a leaf.

"It looks like a strawberry wearing blue jeans," I say, hoping they understand that I mean it as a compliment. From their huge smile, I think it landed right.

Moments like this, when we're not talking about magical destinies or whatever, make everything feel much easier. Still, I keep expecting Dara to suddenly see the real me and run away like the others did.

"Going back to that army," they say. "That would be useful, but imagine, you'd have talk to all of them."

They flash me a cheeky grin, and I laugh. "That sounds worse than the monsters. Maybe we should just have an army of poison dart frogs instead."

"Would you want an army of poison dart frogs or an army of people to blow darts made from their poison?" Dara says, wandering through the exhibit. "Like the frogs are cute but what are they going to do? Lick you? Or maybe they could disarm the monsters with their cuteness!"

Too deep into this frog fantasy, Dara walks smack into Stevie. "Sorry!"

"Watch it," Stevie growls. But under the surface, I can see her fire seems snuffed out. When I'm near her, I feel her worry in my bones like an ache.

The screen she stands at shows a tornado of water called a waterspout, which happens when one passes over the ocean or a really big lake. It's hundreds of metres tall and reminds me far too much of the afanc.

"Are you—" I begin but change tack, or I'll give away that we know Chia is missing. "How did your race go?"

"Fine," she whispers. "After we left you, did you see Chia again?"

"No," blurts Dara. "Is she okay?"

But Stevie doesn't answer. All the energy seeps out of her, and she seems very, very small. "It's my fault," she whispers.

I swear Dara is about to blow our cover and tell her what happened, just as our tour leader appears and gets our attention with one big clap. My nerves jangle at the sudden noise across the low hum of voices.

"Welcome to the climate room," calls Marina, a spindly woman wearing the largest pair of glasses I've ever seen. It's a bit weird to be welcomed, even though we've been standing in here for about ten minutes already. "In here, you can learn all about climate change, greenhouse gases and the weather."

She launches into a lecture she's clearly given many times before about how greenhouse gases warm the planet up. I know a lot about this already. The thing about exhaustion, social isolation, insomnia, and unlimited access to the internet is that you get a lot of reading done. Climate change scared me when I first heard about it, but when I know about a thing, it seems a little less scary.

Marina announces that we've got half an hour of free exploration time before we need to meet up at the lab to do fun experiments.

I pull the folded museum map we printed off the website last night out of my back pocket. It shows we are really close to the steam engines – my favourite bit – but I remember two floors below us there's a big exhibition on space. Astronauts are like the ultimate athlete. You have to be smart and extremely fit to be an athlete. And maybe it would cheer Stevie up.

"Stevie, do you want to come to space with me?"

The firm paper map crinkles in my fingers.

She raises an eyebrow and looks over at me with a face that says *what on earth do you mean.* Her eyes drop to the map. "Oh, the space room? Okay."

And with that, she takes the map from my hands and heads off towards the stairs. It's the most decisive I've seen her be since the park, so I follow behind, not wanting to jinx it.

Dara is barraging Marina with questions about frogs, which she seems delighted to answer, so I just catch their eye and point after Stevie, in the hope that they'll find us later.

We pass through brightly lit corridors, where toddlers on leashed backpacks point and yell, and groups of Mums chatter together. A gaggle of primary school kids race past us waving worksheets and colouring pencils in the air, a multi-coloured streak.

To my relief, the space room is low-lit and quiet.

Every muscle in my body relaxes.

I pass a glowing lit-up globe in the centre of the room and join Stevie by a display of famous astronauts. *Christine Koch, Sally Ride, Mae C. Jemison.* Their photos stand in a big, framed picture.

"I didn't realise there had been so many women astronauts," I whisper. "You only ever see men in films and stuff."

Stevie nods. "You know another thing they all have in common other than being women?"

"What?"

"None of them are disabled," she says flatly, tucking her left arm inside the top of her dungarees.

"I found out the other day that there is *one* disabled astronaut. John McFall, he was a Paralympian. But that's still just one as far as we know. Is your shoulder bothering you today?"

"Yeah," she says, clearly surprised that I noticed. "It's sore from the triathlon. I've got a fin attachment for my little arm for when I swim, and there's one on my bike. But even then, I still push too hard from up here, even on normal days."

"So, it builds up? The ache, I mean."

"Yeah, basically. Thanks, no one ever asks about

it," she says, scuffing her trainer on the shiny floor. "Half the time I feel like people are trying to forget I only have one hand, or they're gawking at me because I opened a jar."

"I get it. People are equally weird with autism," I say, realising this is the first time I've told her I'm autistic. "No one ever knows how to talk about it, and don't want to ask me anything, even if it might help me. Not that I really want to tell people about it all the time, but it is ironic, considering I'm supposed to be the one with communication issues."

A small laugh breaks out of her, and I feel relieved.

"It's tricky because autism isn't visible, unless you know what you're looking for, but it does feel like people would rather ignore that part of me."

"I get it," she says wearily. "It's like that 'ability not disability' stuff, which I don't like either. I'm disabled *and* I can do things. Being disabled isn't a bad thing. It's not one or the other."

"And we spend every day adapting and changing just so we can live in this world," I say. "Actually, that would make us the perfect astronauts."

"You're right. I'm probably stronger and faster than all of them put together." She flexes her biceps.

"And let's be real, as if you wouldn't want a detail-focused autistic running your space mission."

We laugh together and even though she still definitely terrifies me, I feel like I understand her a bit more. We're not friends, which helps drown out the voice in my head screaming about how it's all going to go wrong now I've shown her some of myself.

I take a deep breath and shake the nerves out my fingers. She's not Kelly Keane.

"Thanks for this," Stevie says. "It's nice to know someone who gets it."

Stevie disappears off to the loo, and I am a little relieved. I need a break after that intense conversation, so I go for a wander around the space room.

Off to one side, there's a strange dome-shaped shuttle made of bronze metal. It has a little round window in the door and looks more like vintage diving equipment. The plaque tells me it's called a Soyuz module and took astronauts up to the International Space Station. I can't believe something so small made that huge dangerous journey.

As I stand there reading, a blast of cold runs down my spine, like I'm directly under an air conditioning vent. Except, I'm not.

Without moving my head, I look around me. There's nothing out of the ordinary. Just other people visiting the museum.

And yet, I can't shake the terrible feeling that something is wrong. I flap my hands at my sides, my fingers tapping a beat to get the nerves out.

The smell of rotten eggs fills my nose.

Sulphur, that's what it is.

But I can't tell where it's coming from. It could be from a demonstration somewhere . . .

That's when I see it.

From the corner of my eye, I can see there's something inside the shuttle.

My heart thumps in my chest as I slowly turn to face it, while my brain screams at me to run.

I'm met with a familiar impossible blackness.

And its red eyes are staring right back at me.

Chapter Sixteen

The next thing I know is that I'm on the floor, knocked back as the monster crashes out of the module shuttle.

I'm flat on my back, and I can see it crawling above me on the roof, weaving in between the shuttles hanging from the ceiling.

The Soyuz in front of me rocks ominously on its base, and I scrabble away just in time for it to slam into the ground rather than me. The sound is so loud I feel dizzy.

No one else is in here right now, which is both a good thing and a very bad thing. Good: no one to see the damaged museum property, or to be caught by the monster. Bad: it's literally just me and the creature.

Alarms blare, and I blink hard, trying to adjust to

the noise. The automatic sprinkler system starts up, and soon I'm soaked.

But I can't move. I can't take my eyes off the monster above me. And I know it's watching me.

A voice over the alarm commands visitors to make their way to an exit, and I have to hope that Dara, Stevie and the rest of Science Club follow the advice.

There's too much water everywhere for Dara to use their powers anyway – what worked so well with the afanc would accidentally fry a whole lot of people.

It's up to me.

The monster crawls around on the ceiling, clicking away like an echolocating bat. I wonder what it's looking for, or if it's just taunting me.

Maybe I can lure it away, perhaps trap it in the basement far from everyone else?

Before I can decide, it leaps from the ceiling, legs splayed ready to grab.

But it's not jumping towards me.

Pressed up against the doorway is Stevie. She must've come back for me, and now she is wide-eyed and petrified.

"MOVE!" I screech.

Our eyes meet, and she leaps out of the way, rolling

as she lands hard against the floor.

The monster lands where she was only seconds ago. Its outline pulses like the most twisted toddler's scribble come to life.

I can't tell if it's the same one we saw in the park, which is a horrifying thought on its own: what if there's more than one? What if there are loads of them?

"Get out of here Stevie!"

At my words, the monster turns towards me, red eyes blazing. If they even *are* eyes. It feels like they burn into me. When I blink, I see them imprinted on the inside of my eyelids, like a light I've looked at for too long.

I step back slowly. Goosebumps run up my skin, fear and cold mixing together.

Stevie hesitates, and I'm worried she's going to try and help, so I yell, "Find Dara and get everyone out! I'll distract it."

She seems to accept this and disappears.

As soon as she's out of the way, I pull at the sprinkler water gathering on the floor. I can feel it, under my fingers, and the water starts to swirl, just like the hot chocolate.

It's just the same, I tell myself. It's basically the same. The monster's feet slip in the swirling water, and that's my moment. With one quick jerk, I launch all the water, and the monster with it, into the air away from me.

And with that, I run.

I think back to the map, to the emergency exits, and realise everyone will be running to the edges of the museum. If I work towards the centre, it'll give everyone time to get out.

Crashes sound behind me but I don't look back. All I can hope is that something else fell on it. From the angry, bone-rattling cry that echoes around me, I think I was right.

And now it's really, really angry.

I run into a bright white room and wince at the change in light. Cars stack up against the walls, and planes hang from the ceiling. Each wall is covered in glass cases full of old things. The water still falls from the ceiling, running down the cases like a waterfall.

My trainers are sodden with water and slowing me down, sending huge heavy ripples across the water. I'm just about to take them off when I'm slammed into the floor, again.

This time, it's an information board, ripped from the wall.

And the creature is on top of it.

A dark meaty claw reaches around to grab me, but I wiggle down just out of its reach.

But my relief is short-lived, as the force of it reaching around is pushing my head down into the water, which is rising.

What is it with all these monsters trying to drown me?

I can barely move, but with as much thrust as I can muster, I slam my palm down against the surface of the water like I'm beating a drum.

The water bounces up into the air, taking the display and the monster with it, just long enough for me to scrabble out.

I run, shucking off one trainer that was barely hanging on. Typically, one shoe on and one off is even more annoying than two soggy trainers so I'm running unevenly.

Above me, the creature jumps between the airplanes that hang from the ceiling, chasing me.

With one huge jump, it leaps and scuttles along the wings of a large silver plane, which rocks under its crawling.

I've got a perfect line of sight to it, but as I go to grab at the water, the sprinklers click off.

And the water at my feet drains away.

All that I have left is what's soaked into my single remaining trainer.

And the monster knows it. For something with no obvious face, it looks super pleased.

Disarmed, I race back the way we came. Typical that my talisman is a weapon I couldn't sneak through security, because it'd be really useful right now.

I weave through the chaos of the space room, and dark turns to light again as I sprint back through an open lobby.

The monster is right on my heels, no longer toying with me from the ceiling. I'm by no means a fast runner when not soaked and, given it has somewhere between four and eight legs, this must be an absolute doddle for it. A relaxed jog.

A soda vending machine is up ahead, and as I pass, I yell and slam my hand against it. All the cans of soda inside burst, and the machine cracks open in a shower of metal and fizz. The monster's screech is drowned under the cacophony of a hundred cans bursting at once in a cola bomb.

I keep running through the empty museum. Everyone seems to have gotten out, so maybe it's time for me to bounce too, else this thing is going to absolutely wreck me.

I rush past an enormous steam-powered wheel that takes up the centre of the entrance hall, almost thinking I'm free.

Except, I hear a whimper from the gift shop.

Someone's still here.

I dash inside, crouching down behind the laboratory kits and a very large anatomical model.

Across the shop, I spy two very small, very terrified girls – probably part of the group with the worksheets that ran past me before. One has a long cut down her leg, blood muddying her white tights.

I hold a finger up to my lips, and then beckon them to me.

They hesitate. Hell, if I was them, I wouldn't trust a soaked eleven-year-old to get me out alive either.

The not-bleeding one covers her mouth with her hand, suppressing a scream.

I whip my head round.

Perched on top of the wheel, right opposite the shop, is the monster. Its long ears unfold – it's listening for us.

I want to panic, but I am too afraid it'll hear. I slow my breathing down and repeat my signals to the girls. If they stay low, it shouldn't be able to see them.

We're not far from the front entrance from here. There are no other ways out of the gift shop, but if it gets bored and leaves, we can make a run for it.

We just have to keep quiet.

Slowly, they make their way towards me.

I search the shelves around me for liquids I can use just in case, but there's nothing but sea monkey kits you add water to, which frankly seems like a taunt.

The monster seems to have decided we're not here, its ears retracting back into big circles at the sides of its head. It moves as though it's about to jump down and go back the way we came when a clatter rips through the air.

And its head spins right back towards us.

I whip round to see the girls backing away from a smashed mug.

Plan B time: I lead it back through the museum so they can escape. A buzzing rush of energy floods me as I run out of the gift shop, right at the monster.

"Run to the exit now!" I scream.

Luckily, it takes the bait and follows me. As it jumps down, it cries out and, when I glance over my shoulder, I realise its steps are all over the place. At some point, I must've injured it, but now it seems more intent on killing me.

I run and run and have no idea where I'm going. I just have to make enough time for the girls to get out.

A set of stairs appears at my right, and I scramble up it, which is my first mistake.

I am very uncoordinated at the best of time, and always fall over on stairs. And I'm still wearing one soggy shoe, which makes a horrible squeak as I change direction. My muscles are on fire as I take two steps at a time.

Despite its injury, the beast is just one flight behind me. It's too big and too battered to turn quickly in the stairwell, but it's closing on me.

And I'm slowing down. I've never been a runner; all this is pure adrenalin. Maybe that's another thing I should put on the list to practice if I ever get out of here alive.

I push up the last steps, but I trip on the loose lace of my single shoe, and I land hard, whacking my head as I slide down the steps.

Right towards the monster. It stalks around the corner, and growls with satisfaction, and I'm exhausted. I'm too tired to get up, and part of me wants to give in because it might take me to Chia.

But also, it might rip me apart just for the hell of it.

From nowhere, Stevie appears over me, leaping through the air and swinging a model rocket at the monster. The rocket collides with its head, shattering in an explosion of red and white. The monster howls, sliding down the steps.

Stevie pulls me to my feet and back up the steps, into the room she must've come from. It's a classroom, with a model display in the centre. She climbs up on the table and arms herself with the earth, which looks heavy.

But up ahead, the blackboard looks like it's flickering. The air shimmers, like oil on water.

"What is that?" I whisper, walking over to it.

I reach out to touch it.

And my hand disappears.

It's a doorway, or . . . maybe a portal.

Suddenly, the monster is in the doorway, evading Stevie's shot put.

"I'm out of things to throw Vivi!" she shouts, jumping down beside me.

And there's no other option, even though I'm pretty sure it's the most stupid option.

I grab Stevie, and leap through the portal.

Chapter Seventeen

The portal closes behind us with a gulp, and Stevie and I are left in a cavern. Where the doorway once stood is now solid rock, and I run my hand over it just to be sure. It's damp and cold, but, to my relief, solid.

"I think we're safe," I whisper.

"For now," adds Stevie.

We slide down to the floor in one big exhale.

It's dark in here, but glowing clusters of crystals in the walls cast a soft orange light through the tunnel. I want to touch them and watch the light under my fingers but touching mystery crystals, in a cave I don't know how I got into, seems like a really bad idea. Their light doesn't stretch very far, and I can't see where the exit is, or how far the cave goes, though I presume we're at the very end of it.

For now, I'm just glad that nothing is chasing me.

"You've only got one shoe on," Stevie says.

"Yeah, I lost it a while ago," I say, taking it off.

"So, are you going to finally tell me what's going on?"

My brain completely sticks on the wrong part of her question, and I ask, "What do you mean *finally*?"

"Obviously I've known something was weird about you since we met."

"Most people chalk that up to the autism."

She gives me a hard look. "You know I don't mean that. I mean the water. The almost soaking me, and then not. The messing around on the bench with Dara. The telling me *you've got this* when there's a massive great monster in the middle of the museum."

"The monsters trying to kill me were kind of a giveaway."

"Yeah," she says quietly. "That's what happened to Chia, isn't it?"

"Yeah," I admit. "We don't know what happened, but one grabbed her, and they disappeared. We've been trying to find out where she is and what they are."

"And?"

"No luck yet."

"So, what *have* you been doing?"

"Practicing ways to take them down."

I explain mine and Dara's powers to her, and the inventions Dara had shown me only yesterday, though it feels like a lifetime ago. But then I have to backtrack and explain all the rest – Gelert, Nimuë, Excalibur, Annwn – all the reasons why these monsters keep appearing around us, and why we're suddenly magical. I'm not the best at reading faces, but Stevie's brows seem to furrow deeper and deeper the more we talk.

When I finish, she leans back against the wall and silently takes a very squashed packet from her jacket pocket. She holds it out to me, and I take a flat fruit roll-up gratefully.

After a long quiet, Stevie says, "Your powers are growing, but you don't have the best control over them, am I right?"

I nod, an ache growing in my stomach.

"And you've got a sword, but you haven't had fencing lessons? You don't know how to fight with a sword?"

I blush furiously. "There's no manual for this."

"No, I know," she says. "I was just thinking you need a coach."

This was not what I was expecting to hear.

"I don't know anything about magic, but I know about growing talent and developing it. And you two need an outside person to keep you both on track with that, while you concentrate on getting Chia back."

I'm about to protest, to tell her it's too dangerous, or that I can't decide anything without Dara, but she holds up her hand to stop me.

"No, you don't have a choice. You two zambonis are the only chance we have of getting Chia back, so I'm in. I'm just telling you the benefits of me being part of this little squad."

I have no idea what Gelert is going to say about this, or Dara for that matter, but I just say, "Okay."

"Okay. Now that that's sorted, let's work out where we are."

Stevie stands and helps me to my feet. I've calmed down enough from the imminent threat of the monster that my muscles have cooled down, and I'm stiff. It's going to hurt later.

"A cave," I say exhausted. "A big damp cave."

"Huh," Stevie says, wiping a finger down the wall. A bead of murky water rests on her fingertip. "Maybe we should take some of this with us."

"Some of what?"

I expect Stevie to point out how stupid I'm being for not paying attention, but she just holds up the fruit roll-up packet. "Can you pull some of the water from the walls into this? That way, if something happens, you've got some ammo."

"I can try." Normally, if I was this tired, I'd be wrapped up in bed destimming, but the wobble in Stevie's voice wakes me up. We have no idea what's in here with us, and I'm the only one with magic.

My hand shakes as I reach out for the water, and I feel the pull, even if it's as dull and slow as my thoughts feel. Slowly, very slowly, drops of water run across the walls of the cave, gathering like a snowball getting bigger. They fall into the packet, held open in Stevie's hand, until there's about a mug of water in there.

"That's all I can do," I say.

Stevie nods and hands me the packet, which I clutch against my chest, hoping I don't spill it. "Good work."

"Is it?"

"They say you can drown in a few teaspoons of water."

Before I can ask how she knows this, she leads

me through the cave. We walk slowly, keeping our bodies close to one wall.

But the cave keeps going and going. It takes me a moment, but I realise we're not in a simple dead-end cave, like the ones in the cliffs near home. We are in a tunnel. Crystals erupt from the wall and ceiling, lighting our way through the gloom.

We see no one else, but I still wish I had Excalibur with me. Anything more than a snack packet full of dirty water.

"Do you think Dara is okay?" Stevie whispers, but before I can answer she backtracks, a furious blush on her cheeks. "Never mind."

"I'm sure they're okay," I say after a few more steps. "I wish they were here."

"Is it weird we haven't seen anyone?" she asks instead.

"I don't really want to jinx it. But yeah, I haven't even seen any bugs or anything you'd expect in a cave."

Stevie shivers. "I'm kind of okay with that."

We keep walking in silence. I've no idea how long we've been walking but I'm tired and my bare feet are filthy. All we can do is keep going.

Up ahead, the tunnel opens up, and I can see the path splitting. One gigantic cluster of crystals stands in the centre like a waypoint.

A rattle cuts through the air.

Stevie drags me flat against a curve in the wall, and instinctively I hold my breath.

Coming out of a tunnel into the crossroads is one of the monsters. I've never seen any of them just going about their day; they've only ever been hunting or actively trying to kill me.

But this one saunters along around the crystal cluster, touching its horrible spidery legs along it as it walks past. It's small, but I still don't fancy taking my chances with it. Especially not with just a packet of water.

We watch it turn down one of the tunnels up ahead.

I breathe out finally.

And that's when it looks up and freezes in its tracks.

My eyes grow wide as I realise it has, somehow, worked out we're here.

Slowly, ever so slowly, it starts to turn. It hasn't seen us yet.

I want to ready the water in my hand just in case, but I know that if I do, the packet will crinkle; we'll definitely be in trouble then.

We don't move, we barely breathe, and, after what

feels like an eternity, it leaves for good.

Stevie and I stay flat against that wall for a long time, not daring to move. When we finally drop to the floor, hopeful that we're safe for now, our exhausted muscles shake.

Stevie places a finger over her lips and then signals to the floor. She mouths the word *rest*. We can't stay here long, as anything could come down those tunnels.

As we sit, I quietly dig a symbol in the muck of the wall. An infinity symbol, to mark that we'd been down this path. There's so many up ahead, and who knows how they link back together. I don't want to accidentally end up at this dead end again.

As I dust the dirt off my fingers, someone speaks. Someone who isn't Stevie or me; it isn't a voice I've heard before.

"Well, well, well. Two little adventurers who've lost their way."

Chapter Eighteen

Of all the things in this tunnel, I didn't expect to find a teenage boy. He's older than us – he has that skinny, too-long, not-grown-into-yourself look that Mr. Bevan's son Geraint morphed into last year. But, other than that, he doesn't look anything like Geraint. For a start, he's wearing a cape.

Stevie cuts eyes at him, and presses a finger repeatedly against her lips, telling him to shut up.

"Oh, do not fear. They cannot hear us. For now."

"Ominous," I mutter under my breath, which gets a quiet nod from Stevie.

He reclines against the crystals as though they're a huge comfortable chair, and when I look closer, I can see they *have* changed shape, moulding underneath his body. I want to ask him who he is, but

I'm too nervous, the packet crinkling under my fingers that want to flick.

We stand, but Stevie steps in front of me. "Who are you?"

"You may call me . . . Emrys," he says, as though it was a whim rather than his name.

"Okay Emrys, *where* are we?" asks Stevie.

"Do you not know?"

I kind of hate this smug guy's vibe.

"Clearly not," Stevie snaps. Clearly, she dislikes this guy as much as me.

He chuckles, and I'm not convinced that he's not laughing at us. "Why, you are in the Unlands."

The Unlands.

"Of course," I whisper. Gelert had told me about the Unlands just after Chia was taken. What had he called it? A place to travel through. I relay what Gelert told me to Stevie, whose eyes widen at the realisation that we are not even in our world anymore.

"Ah, this adventurer is not so lost then?" Emrys asks.

"Oh no, we are definitely still lost," Stevie sighs.

Knowing where we are doesn't fill me with much hope, unless Gelert manages to find us here. It's just us, this weird boy, and possibly a whole heap of monsters.

"What are you doing here then?" Stevie asks.

"The same as you, the same as all. I'm just passing through."

"Is that what those monsters are doing? Passing through?"

"Which *monster* do you speak of?" he asks, in a way that makes me worry that there are other things we should be scared of in here.

"That creepy spider thing."

"Ah, the first plague," he says, with an eyeroll.

A plague? My mind runs through the things I know associated with plague: London, the weird bird masks that the doctors wore, a sweeping sickness that meant doors were marked. Or the plague of locusts from the stories of Egypt – but while these monsters are a bit buggy and can jump far, they aren't locusts.

Then it comes to me. Like the parrots in London, I realise, or those furry clawed crabs. "Do you mean they're like an invasive species?" I croak.

And the boy smiles.

"Perhaps," he says, in a very annoying cryptic way.

We wait for him to elaborate, but he does not. It's obvious we're not going to get any more out of him about the monsters that seem very keen on catching children.

"Do you know a way out?" Stevie asks him.

"That depends on where you want to go."

Beside me, I can feel how agitated Stevie is – it radiates off her like heat. I still her with a hand, not taking my eyes off the strange boy. I choose my words carefully. I've read enough stories where creatures trick you if you're not clear enough, or if you leave any wiggle room. (And I thought talking to most humans was bad enough.)

"We want to go back to the human world, specifically back to our London in the UK."

He raises an eyebrow. "It is wise of you to be so precise."

This is when I realise that the whole time we've been speaking he's had a long curved staff next to him. He picks it up and points it down one of the tunnels.

"If you go that way, you will find your way back to your world. There is a portal open, and it should hold. But don't linger if you can help it."

"Thank you," I say.

He might not be willing to tell us everything, but it's clear Emrys knows more than we do about the Unlands. I can't let this opportunity to find out more go. "Can I ask you another question?"

"That depends more on whether you can speak or not, surely?" he says in a way that I think is particularly smelly.

I try to suppress an eyeroll. Stevie doesn't even try to.

"Vivi, let's just go. He's too weird," she whispers, but I shake my head.

"If I ask another question about the Unlands, will you answer truthfully?"

He smiles again. "As you've entertained me so, I shall."

I take a moment to find the right words.

"As these tunnels and therefore the Unlands lie alongside our world, could we use these tunnels to travel across our country in the same way that the monsters are doing?"

"Oh, you are a clever one," he says with a smile. I'm not the best at reading facial expressions of people I know, never mind mysterious people I find in other dimensions, but he seems genuinely pleased. "Yes, you are right, little water witch. Provided you have the means to travel and are able to avoid the dangers here, then yes, you could navigate through your world by these tunnels. If you can open the portals. You must know that time and space work a little differently here, but it is possible to follow the crystals. While the tunnels may twist and turn, you can be sure of your path by the colours."

I take another look around us and realise there are different coloured crystals here. Blue and orange, like those we've been following this whole time, but also green and pink.

"Are these directional?" I ask.

He raises his eyebrows and I take that to mean *yes*.

"But I must warn you adventurers, beware of words you hear. There are truths and there are lies, and you can be sure of nothing in the Unlands."

"Okay," I say, trying to commit this painfully unclear warning to memory. "Are you coming with us?"

"No," he says, and, with that, he gets up and walks down a different tunnel. He's gone.

"What a weird guy," I whisper just in case the monsters are near

"Why was he wearing a cape? And that staff. He looked like someone wearing a wizard fancy-dress costume."

"Yeah. He did," I say, biting the soft skin on the inside of my lip.

I swear I've heard the name Emrys before, but I can't think where, or when. It must have been from one of Mumma's stories, though there's no guarantee it's the same person.

Either way, I feel weird about that conversation. More than I usually do.

"Are they all like that?" Stevie mutters between clenched teeth, as we walk down the path he pointed to. "Talking in circles and riddles?"

"Oh yes," I say. "Getting a simple answer out of them is like getting blood from a stone."

"That must be hard for you," she says, and I'm kind of grateful that she noticed. It *is* hard. It takes so much brain power for me to follow normal conversation, never mind these weirdly vague proclamations from mysterious people, or dogs, from other realms.

"We should have asked him if he'd seen Chia," I groan, kicking myself.

"I don't think he'd have given us a straight answer even if he had."

This tunnel is much wider than the one we first

found ourselves in, and quickly it opens up into a massive cavern. When I can, I pause to draw an infinity symbol to mark our way. The cavern must be extremely tall, because the crystals that must be on the ceiling are small pinpricks. It's weird; like walking into a ballroom, but it just keeps going. And going.

It's lit well enough that we don't have to trace a wall, but Stevie and I still stick close together.

The walls continue to fall away, and it feels even less like we're in a room. It's more like we're in a void. I am not a fan.

And that's when we hear someone calling for us.

"Stevie? Vivi? Help me!"

It's Dara. How can Dara be here? The portal closed behind us, so they couldn't have come in.

Could the monster have gotten them after we'd escaped?

"Stevie," I whisper, remembering Emrys' warning.

But her grip on me tightens, and she speeds up, dragging me after her. "We have to get Dara."

The tunnel narrows dramatically, and, while it continues ahead, there's a pathway jutting off to the side.

"Guys, please!" they cry, their voice echoing down this small tunnel.

I quickly mark the dirt as Stevie charges down the tunnel. I try not to spill any water as I trot to keep up. The tunnel winds and curls, reminding me of rabbit burrows.

And then again, we're in a big wide cavern, and the voice is gone.

"I swear this is where we were before," she growls.

"It is," I say, pointing at the floor where a scuffed infinity symbol is drawn in the dirt. We walked right over it.

"Is that one of yours?"

"I hope so, or we're in bigger trouble than I thought."

"Well, either Dara is in here or we're being led around in circles by something else, so I'd say we're already pretty stuffed."

As if in answer, a rattle cuts across the cavern, and up ahead I can see four red glowing eyes.

We can't run – if we do, we risk going in circles – and we can barely fight. But, that's the only option we have.

For a moment, the monster and I stand eye to eye. Those burning red eyes that haunt my dreams.

But I can't move. I can't do anything. The water is

just like regular, before magic, water to me. And I think the monsters knows. It starts to advance on us very slowly.

"Vivi," whispers Stevie. "Now would be a really great time to do something."

My stomach squirms with shame. I just want to be a normal kid; not facing off against a monster in some parallel universe or whatever.

"Vivi, stop being a coward," snaps Stevie. "You can't just do nothing!"

And this snaps something in me. This has nothing to do with her; it's about whether *Dara and I* can save Chia and stop this mysterious King from nerfing our world, never mind just stopping the monster in front of me.

Bubbling heat runs through my body, and I thrash, feeling a hum run through me. She doesn't have to live this. I do.

And with that, the water from the packet curls into my hand forming a perfect sphere of water.

Realising that something has changed, the monster charges forward, and I launch the water with all my might.

With all my furious energy, I sweep the water at

its legs.

The monster wobbles off course, and we leap out of the way as it crashes into the wall. Just as I'm readying myself to call the water back, the monster runs away.

I only drop the water when Stevie pats my shoulder.

I don't know where the water goes. I can't feel it anymore, so it's either too far away for me to pull back, or I'm too tired.

"Anger," she says quietly.

"Sorry?"

"Okay, so don't be mad, but I had a feeling that your emotions might be connected to the water. And because anger is the biggest feeling, you get the biggest response. It's like your energy source, a mental state you need to tap into. Like when I'm running, and I just focus on how everyone will look when I beat them."

"Wow."

"You're mad."

"I don't appreciate being provoked," I growl at her, "but you're right."

"Sorry, I just needed to test the theory," she says, distinctly not sorry. "But now we know for sure, your emotions are the key to your powers."

I hate that she's right. Emotions are overwhelming to me; I feel them in every single bit of my body, like an ache or even like pain. I used to try not to feel them, but that just made things worse. And I hate that now I apparently have to let myself feel all that, rather than ignoring it, in order to use my magic.

"Do you think Dara is really in here too?" I ask.

"No. I think it was a trick. Let's just focus on getting out of here," she says, leading the way. She's right. There's nothing we can do to help Chia with basically no plan, no weapons, and no idea where we are.

This time, we don't turn off and go back on ourselves, and we take the other tunnel. There are clusters of blue crystals down this tunnel.

Just as Emrys said there would be, there's a portal.

"Ready?" she asks, holding her hand out to me.

I take it, and we step through.

With a rush, we are through, and standing in the middle of a park. The portal doesn't close behind us, but it dims and becomes harder to see.

The sun is very low in the sky – we must have been in there basically the whole school day. There's an information sign next to us, and Stevie pulls me over to it, still gripping my hand. The wind whips at our clothes but I'm thankful for the fresh air.

"I know where we are," she says. "We're back in London. In fact, we're a tram ride away from home."

"Oh my days, we found you!"

We're both knocked off balance by Dara, who pulls us into the biggest hug.

After what seems like an allowed time length, I wriggle free of Dara's death grip. Stevie and Dara don't let go of each other, but I guess non-autistic people just like hugs.

"How did you find us?" I say, and Dara and Stevie spring apart, their cheeks flushed.

"I tracked you, didn't I?" says Gelert, who nuzzles my arm. "Smelled you the minute you popped out of that." He inspects the portal, sniffing all around it.

"Are you guys okay?" Dara asks. "I was so worried when you were both missing."

"We're okay," Stevie says with a smile. "Vivi kept me safe."

"It was definitely more of a collaboration," I say.

"I can't believe you went into a portal," says Dara. "And, erm, I'm guessing you know about everything now huh?"

Stevie just nods. This is a conversation for another day.

"Is it still open?" Dara asks.

"Yeah," Stevie says. "Look."

She puts her head through, disappearing into the air, and then pulls back quickly. "I don't think it's going to close."

"Woahhhh. Wait, that means there's an open active portal near to us . . ." Dara says.

Their words hang in the air. The monsters could come back, I realise. Very easily.

"Come on," says Stevie. "I know the way home."

"I'll stay to look around," announces Gelert, returning to his sniffing.

Too tired to think any more, I follow Dara and Stevie without question, glad to be back in our world with normal things like grass and pigeons and other humans walking their dogs.

Chapter Nineteen

Honestly, the worst part of this magical destiny stuff is that I still have to go to school. I'm so tired this morning that I consider drinking some of Mam's foul-smelling coffee; I basically have to drag myself to the front gates.

Luckily, I'd gotten home last night around the same time that the school trip was supposed to be back, so my Mums were none the wiser. I just had to keep them away from any news reports about the Science Museum, which luckily seemed to have been chalked up to one of those rare British earthquakes mixed with a faulty sprinkler system.

The three of us planned to meet in the stuffy little library room before school. We'd been too tired to talk about what we'd been through on the way home.

Dara is already there when I arrive, relief splashed across their face. "I was worried you'd have disappeared again."

"Luckily not," I say.

While we wait for Stevie, we look through the shelves, in case any of those books happen to be about myths, but unfortunately none of them are remotely useful. Lots of barely held-together paperbacks about summer romances.

"Nothing on myths, but I think we'll be experts in kissing after all this," mutters Dara, sliding a book back onto its shelf.

"Why are you in here talking about kissing?" Stevie asks. At this, Dara's ears go pink.

Before that awkward moment can continue, Gelert appears, settling himself on the floor. I hope no one comes in and sees a huge dog is here.

"Does he always do that?" Stevie asks.

"Sleep?" asks Dara.

"Just . . . appear."

"Oh! Yeah, he does that."

"Hang about," Gelert raises his huge head and stares at Stevie, as though this is the first time he's noticed her. "Who's this again?"

"This is Stevie, Gelert," Dara says. "You met her last night. She came out of the portal with Vivi."

"Hmm," he murmurs. Not quite a growl, but it's throaty. "I'm not sure about a non-calon knowing about all this. Can we not wipe her memory?"

"Absolutely not!" shrieks Dara. "Wait . . . you can do that?"

"Honestly, I don't think I'd mind forgetting that much," laughs Stevie.

"We're not wiping her memory Gelert," I say, trying to sound assertive. "Stevie's going to help us train with our powers and get stronger – she already helped me see that my emotions affect my powers."

"I think she'll be a great member of our team," adds Dara.

"Tell me, girl," he says, approaching her. "Where do you see yourself here? Without magic, you'll always be in danger. I can't guarantee your safety."

Stevie stands straighter, and immediately I see the confidence she must use for her races. "Their job is to find the missing children, including Chia, and fight the monsters and stop this whole magical world disaster from happening, right? Well, they need someone on their case to make sure they're training.

I know the discipline it takes to make a body stronger. They need to focus on their own talents, and any time spent on training each other is time lost. Plus, they're all too nice to point out if one of them is slacking; it's going to hold them both back."

"She's not wrong," sniffs Gelert.

"I'm not cut out to be mean," whispers Dara.

"I'm not mean. I'm constructive," she says. "Perhaps like, 5% mean, just to motivate you."

"The point is, I'm probably the best hope you've got and if I don't help you improve, then you can just fire me or wipe my memory or whatever."

An uncomfortably long time passes as Gelert sizes her up. And then, he just lies back on the floor. "Seems an alright sort to me. I'll allow it."

"The official seal of approval," says Dara, who seems relieved.

"Wow, what an honour." Stevie picks long grey hairs off her trousers with a grimace. "What would have happened if he'd said no?"

"Probably would have eaten you or something," he says without opening an eye. Stevie freezes and Gelert bursts out laughing, extremely pleased with himself.

"Sorry, he's very annoying," I say.

"Something you all have in common," she sighs, and turns to Dara. "I should have guessed you had some kind of magic going on, based on the number of times you've given me a static shock this year."

"Ah, yeah, sorry about that. It happens when I'm nervous."

She raises a brow at this but ignores it. "So, what next? How are we going to save Chia, first of all."

"We go back to the Unlands," Dara says. "If we can map it out, we can find her more easily. If there are open portals over the city—"

"—We could use them to get around and find out where the monsters are going," she finishes.

"Bingo."

"Hang on," I say. "We need to find out what those monsters are first. The Unlands were crawling with them."

"Literally," shudders Stevie. "But how are we going to do that?"

I pull my tablet out of my rucksack and explain *Strange Britain* to them, which Stevie is understandably a little sceptical of. Dara manages to get me onto the school WiFi, having apparently charmed the password out of the secretary already, and they crowd around me as I show them the website.

Annoyingly, our last comment about the monsters has no replies. They've already moved on – unsurprisingly to the events of the Science Museum.

It seems that our suspicions about the shadows targeting children might be correct. Along with Clare Woodfine, commenters have alerted me to the mysterious kidnappings of Jason Ortega and now Isabella Valente – another familiar story of disappearing from a South London park.

We also have reason to suspect that the activity at the Science Museum might be related, with a single eyewitness account from this Facebook post by @kmbalia mentioning a large shadow, chalked up by the normies to be an earthquake.

But we're much, much smarter than they are.

And so, my darling ones, I appeal to you. We must solve this mystery, before any more children go missing.

The comments are full of discussions about psychic blasts and spectral disturbances. Two regulars have been arguing about the possibilities of pretty much everything, from dormant buried dragons to a kelpie infestation. As usual, not quite right.

"These people move fast," says Dara.

"Yeah, quickly in the wrong direction," scoffs Stevie.

I add a new comment at the bottom and start writing.

"What are you doing?" says Stevie. "You aren't speaking to these people, are you?"

"I've written before but what if no one replied because I was new, and they thought we were just pranking them? Let's just give it one more try."

"Can't hurt more I guess," she sighs.

I log in and add a comment to the bottom of the post.

nimuë&ceridwen *commented:*

Dear Ghost Queen,
We were at the Science Museum and can confirm all the above. We want to rescue the stolen children and we need your help. We have faced off against the monsters a number of times. We have heard them referred to as "a plague."

"Now what?" asks Dara.

I shrug. "We wait."

"Let's meet after school," says Stevie. "We've got planning to do."

*

Stevie wasn't joking about planning.

On her lap is a notebook, with a pink sequin cover, that catches the sunlight, refracting it around us. *Dara* and *Vivi* are written at the top of the two open pages, along with notes scribbled in a bright turquoise gel pen that she must have got from Chia.

I settle down on the chair next to her and pull out my tablet.

"What is all this?" asks Dara, peering over Stevie's shoulder.

"It's so I can track your progress. I already know what Vivi can do, or some of it. Speaking of which, you and I need a training session, Dara."

"OK!" they almost-shout, ears pink.

Stevie asks them to explain their powers and makes copious notes in her book.

My tablet is a bit old, so it takes a while to load. But when it does, there's something strange. An email notification. I haven't given anyone my email address since I moved, and even then, no one ever emailed me.

Right at the top of my inbox is an unread email from 'Your Friend'.

It must be spam, but curiosity gets the better of me, and I open it. But this is no spelling error riddled spam email from someone trying to steal the £5 in my bank account.

It's an email from the Ghost Queen.

"Guys," I whisper, but they don't hear me, too busy bickering about what conducts electricity. "GUYS."

"What?" snaps Stevie.

"She wrote back."

"Who?"

"We've got a lead," I whisper.

"Alright, Detective Conway," she snorts, but they both get up to read the email over my shoulder.

> Dear Nimuë and/or Ceridwen,
> I believe that I have found the way to answer your question. Do you wish to know more?
> Your friend in mischief,
> The Ghost Queen

"Woah, how did she get your email?" Dara asks,

squeezing into the chair next to me.

I open a new email and reply.

Yes I want to know more. Nimuë.

The only sound is my heart thumping in my chest as we wait for her reply. And it comes in seconds, but it's not an email. It's an instant message from the program attached to my email that I never use.

Hello Nimuë.

"This is all a bit bloody weird, isn't it?" huffs Gelert. His great head rests on my knee.

Hello.
What did you find out?

She doesn't reply.

Can I trust you?

That depends.
You can trust me to not share anything you tell me

here about yourself, or your friends.

We all glance at each other nervously at 'your friends.'

But any further information we uncover pertaining to the creatures in question will be shared. Information shouldn't be ring-fenced; this is an open scientific community.

"What does that mean?" sniffs Stevie.

"She wants to be able to talk about it on *Strange Britain* I guess," I say.

"I'm not sure about scientific," says Dara.

Okay.

You spoke of a plague. Who told you this?

I look at the others. Do I tell her?

On one hand, I might be sharing information that could help us find out what they are. On the other, I could be telling all my otherworldly secrets to a stranger on the internet.

I look at Dara, and they nod, eyes eager.

And so, that's how I ended up telling the Ghost

Queen about the Unlands, and Emrys.

"Emrys?" says Gelert suddenly. "Did you write Emrys?"

"Yeah, why?"

"That name . . ." he says, searching his memory. "There was a mountain, but first a man. And . . ." He growls with frustration.

"It'll come to you. Give it time," I say, and he huffs hot air. Sometimes my meltdowns play with my memory, and I know how frustrating it can be. You just have to wait.

I believe the answer you seek can be found here.

And what follows are a series of numbers and letters, that look like complete garbage. Followed by an address for . . .

The British Library. In the basement, if you follow these directions, you will find the text I believe you are looking for.

And nowhere else has it?

It's an out-of-print pamphlet from 1904.

In short, no.

But you must go at night. You won't be able to reach the archives in the day.

An email appears in my inbox from the Ghost Queen, with information about how the British Library stores their books in huge basement rooms, plus a map that I'm almost certain is not publicly available.

Stevie scribbles the numbers and letters down at the back of her notebook. She tears the page out, gives it to Dara, and then makes another copy.

And you can't go?

No.

But I'm sure such an adventure would be no difficulty for a great witch and the lady of the lake.

Well, she had us there.

What's in this pamphlet?

The truth of these monsters, if I'm right.

It may connect them to the plagues I'm thinking of.

Good luck.

"How are we going to get there," I say. "I don't think my Mums are going to be down with me going to the British Library in the middle of the night."

"The portal," says Stevie. "Emrys told us we could navigate our world through the Unlands. It's time to go exploring."

Chapter Twenty

The plan was this: go home, get some rest, pack a bag, and sneak out at midnight. Gelert would coordinate on making sure we all met up.

I sleepwalk through the rest of the school day, and by the time I get home I don't even have to try to fall asleep.

When I wake, it's getting dark.

Mam's head is poking round the door. "Come on, sleepy head. You need to get some food in you."

Her knocking must have woken me up, and good thing too – I'm so tired that I feel weighed down, like I'm on a planet with stronger gravity.

I rub sleep out of my eyes and follow her down to the kitchen. Mumma places a bowl of peanut butter noodles in front of me. The smell of my comfort food makes me feel a bit more awake. The sour lime drizzled on top tickles my nose.

"So, how are things going?" asks Mam, delicately picking noodles up with chopsticks.

"Okay," I say, shovelling food into my mouth and coming alive again with every bite.

Mumma makes a small, excited noise.

"And . . . everything's ok?" Mam asks cautiously.

"With what?"

"School, peanut."

"Oh, yeah, it's fine. I'm just really tired."

"And Dara is being a friend to you?" Mam asks cautiously. *Please say you aren't getting bullied again* is what she means, and not in a bad way. She knows it wasn't my fault. I just know the Mums are so hopeful that this new start is working.

I set down my fork, my bowl now completely empty. "They are, I promise."

Not really sure why I promised that at the end. Who knows if things will stay the same – the others certainly started off nice or I thought they were. I ignore the gurgle in my stomach that could be anxiety or the result of scarfing down a whole bowl of noodles in just a few minutes.

"Good. And remember we're both here too," adds Mumma.

"I know," I say.

Truthfully, I probably would tell them if I started getting bullied again. But the problems I have now are strictly not for the parents.

As I get up to clear my plate, I spot my Mums sharing the same hopeful look. I excuse myself, putting my bowl in the dishwasher, claiming I need an early night. Which is true, I really do. Unfortunately, that's not what I'm going to get tonight.

Packing for an adventure in another world isn't so easy, but I put in a torch, a bottle of water, some snacks, a ball of wool from Mam's stash I know she won't miss, and Excalibur. I've not been able to take it with me before, and I know Stevie wants me to learn how to use a sword properly. It's heavy in my hand.

Once the Mums have gone to sleep, I slip out from under the covers. Gelert appears, right on cue, to blip me out of the house so I don't have to use the door. Outside, Stevie is already there.

"Did he get you first?"

"Oh, no. My parents are away," she says quietly.

"What's that?" I say, realising she's holding

something.

It's a shiny metal baseball bat.

She shrugs. "Seemed stupid not to arm myself too."

We walk round the corner to Dara's, and they slip out of the back gate. Gelert couldn't blip them out, or Callie would start barking. Luckily, they're more sneaky than me.

I never really went out on my own in the evenings in Wales because I lived in the middle of nowhere, and when it was dark, it was really dark. But here, the streetlights are still lit, and delivery drivers cycle past. The city is still awake.

Hopefully our parents aren't.

We get to the park quickly, and Dara undoes the lock on the gates with their awl. Stevie leads us straight back to the portal; I was so tired when we got back that I barely registered where it was, so it's lucky she remembered.

She sticks her head through, and then turns back to us. "It's all clear."

"So, what's the plan?" Dara asks.

"I have a theory about how to get around," I say. "Emrys told us that the crystals were directional. When we were travelling, we only saw orange and blue crystals, and then right at the end only blue. But there were others. I think the blue ones must grow in the South."

"You think they're related to parts of London?" Dara says, their eyes wide. "I mean, that would track, to find a mix in the middle. The Science Museum isn't far from the river. Maybe it's like when river water mixes with saltwater in estuaries, so they blend together."

"And there were green ones," adds Stevie.

"When?" I ask.

"Right at the beginning when we got in there. There were a few, but they were really tiny."

"Okay," I say. "So, we need to follow orange ones only. If we can."

I explain my infinity symbol markers from last time, but quickly realise we can't use the same symbol this time or we could get confused if the old markers are still there.

"I'll draw a butterfly this time," Dara says, spinning their awl between their fingers.

"That'll take too long," Stevie says.

"I've got the awl. I choose the symbol."

"Fine."

"Any final words?"

"Wow, I'm so relieved we have you to be our motivation," they laugh.

"Let's stick together," I say. "And . . . stay alert."

Dara notes the time: twenty minutes past midnight. And then, hands in a chain, we step through together.

I'm still not used to the weird rushing of going through a portal. It reminds me of when you dive into a pool, and all the water rushes past you, except I can't *see* anything moving past me.

We are back in the same, blue-lit tunnel.

"Woah," whispers Dara completely in awe.

They make a tiny spark in their hand, brightening our path. Purple melts into blue, and we're cast in an eerie glow.

I'm scared but I go first, seeing as I'm the one who has this theory about where we are going. Dara follows me, then Stevie, followed by Gelert.

We move slowly, one quiet step at a time. I'm so determined not to make a sound that, after almost no time, my muscles ache with the tension of holding myself together.

Soon, we are back at the point where the tunnel turns into the enormous cavern. Dara marks a butterfly on the wall with their awl.

Gelert slips past us, scouting ahead, and quickly returns, ushering us on.

Luckily, we seem to be alone. For now, at least.

Up ahead, I find the old tunnel we had come from, and we walk down it to the crossroads where Emrys was. He's not here today; probably for the best, I'm not sure I have any remaining brain for cryptic clues.

There's no sign of Chia either. I wonder how far through the Unlands she is from us, if she's even here.

One of the tunnels, next to the one marked with an infinity from last time, is solid orange, and seems a good choice as any.

"Wait," whispers Stevie. "Did you hear that?"

"Hear what?" Dara asks, as I shake my head.

"Nothing," she says. "I must have imagined it."

"Let's keep going," I say.

We walk. And walk.

The thing they don't tell you about adventuring in unknown lands is that it soon becomes kind of boring. I mean, not entirely, because we were constantly on the lookout for something about to kill us, but following crystals through empty tunnels when you're half asleep and can't really talk or hum or anything . . .

That's about the point that I start to get suspicious about the lack of monsters following us.

Eventually, the path splits in two, both as orange as each other.

At once, Stevie and Gelert point to the same tunnel and say, "That way."

"How do you know?" I ask.

Stevie shrugs, and Gelert sniffs the air. "Smells right."

The weirdest bit is they were right. Up ahead is a portal, the edges crusted with orange crystals, and when we peek our heads out, we're by a river. No, a canal.

"Is this the right place?" I ask, as we all hop out. We're in the middle of a gigantic circular structure that's creaking with the ever-present blustering gale.

Luckily, the portal doesn't shut behind us.

"Regent's Canal. These are the old gas towers," says Dara, who shakes their watch. The hands suddenly move, aligning themselves at twenty to one.

"We were definitely walking for more than twenty minutes," says Stevie, and part of me wants to ask how she knows, but of course she knows. She's Stevie. "I think that means time is at least twice as fast in there. Good to know."

We all glance back at the portal and I know we're all thinking of Chia.

"So, how far is the British Library?" I ask, keeping my voice low.

"Close," says Dara. "Come on, it's this way."

We walk along the canal, over a bridge, and down past the train station towards a huge redbrick building.

"I was thinking," begins Stevie, and I know in my bones I'm going to hate this conversation just from the airy way she starts it. "You know how you can use water and stir your hot chocolates and whatever. I wonder if that means you can use any form of water, like ice or even mist."

"I've stopped water from moving but not *frozen* it," I say.

"You are really good at stirring up a hot chocolate," adds Dara. "I wonder if you can use other stuff, like soup. Or gravy."

"Well," snorts Stevie. "I was thinking more along the lines of blood."

A shiver runs through my body. "Um, I don't want to think about whether I can control blood," I say, feeling like I'm going to be sick. The logic bit of my brain that likes to throw out facts reminds me that blood plasma is 90% water.

"That's quite villainy," says Dara, clearly also as freaked out as I am. "Way more so than gravy."

"We shouldn't rule it out, though do we even know if these monsters have blood? If she can use blood, maybe you could use the electricity in bodies. Like from the nerves?"

"Are you hearing yourself?" Dara gasps, whose pale skin is somehow paler. "This is *proper* villainy."

"Alright, it does sound a little villainy," she concedes. "But you can't be wusses about this. We've got to be smarter than them, think about every angle you can use."

"Let's just focus on this, please. Or Dara and I are going to pass out before we get there," I say, snakes squirming in my stomach. I wish I was a normal kid worrying about school or Fortnite instead of breaking into libraries and magically controlling someone's blood.

I have only ever been to one library before – a tiny

rickety single-level building in the next town over in Wales that seemed to be as old as any of the castles nearby. The roof would rattle in any breeze, and it always smelt of dust and musty pages whatever the weather. A nice lady called Susan with thick blonde hair and owly glasses would sometimes let me use the old date stamp.

So, even though I obviously looked it up before we came here, I'm still surprised just *how* big the building is. And that's what we can see. The information from the Ghost Queen means there's even more, right under our feet.

"Get as close as you can," says Gelert. "And I'll take you in one at a time."

We sneak around the building to a big courtyard, where glass-fronted doors reveal a huge white marble lobby. An enormous column of backlit books runs through the heart of the building. I want to press my nose against the glass and read all the titles.

Flat against the wall, the three of us peak through the doors while Gelert scouts around the building.

"Can you see anyone?" Dara whispers.

"No," says Stevie. "But that doesn't mean there aren't security guards or cameras inside."

"I can deal with the cameras."

"Can you?" I ask.

"I've been practicing. I think I can turn them off, and if I can't, I'll fry them."

"That doesn't sound reassuring."

"Please do not start a fire," groans Stevie. "No more sprinkler systems."

Gelert returns and takes Dara first. I see them reappear on a mezzanine above the lobby, next to the wall of books. Stevie goes next, and by the time it's my turn, Gelert looks exhausted.

"Are you sure you're up to this?" I ask, but he doesn't respond, just whizzes me through the seams of the world into the library.

"Don't you worry about me," he sniffs. Before I can say anything else, he says, "I'll patrol," and disappears down the steps.

There's a fizz and a pop, and I look up to see Dara fry a security camera above us. It sags on its hinges, and I feel a little bad that we're damaging a public library.

"Come on, there's a staircase right over there," Stevie whispers.

We go through a door so heavy that all three of

us have to hold onto it as it shuts, so it closes softly. The staircase is a huge echoey square. I peek over the side, but it only goes a few floors down. This must be as far as you can go as a visitor.

We reach a door that says 'No Public Access' and I check the map the Ghost Queen sent us. We're going the right way. It's an old wooden door with a modern lock on it.

Dara places their hands over the metal panels on the door, and I can taste the electricity in the air. The door slackens, and I know it's open.

"That's so cool," I whisper.

"You are surprisingly useful," says Stevie with a smile.

Dara coughs awkwardly. "Shall we go in?"

On the other side of the door is a barely lit corridor, the white paint marked and peeling; the automatic lights that flick on as we pass all seem to be running out, their light weak and orange.

"I always expect behind the scenes to be cool and fancy, but it always looks like this," sighs Dara.

We come to another staircase and start walking down. I cling to the banister hoping it might hold me up.

"How deep does this go?" Stevie murmurs.

"24 metres according to Ghost Queen's info," I say. "Like an eight-storey building, only going down."

"Why do I find this place even creepier than the Unlands?" she says with a shudder.

"It's because you hate books," laughs Dara, and she swats them.

I look at the map, and we seem to be going the right way. Just one more floor down.

Which is just as I hear a rattle echoing up the core of the stairs.

We all freeze at once, eyes wide.

One of them is here.

I peer over the side, down the centre of the stairs, and right at the bottom, lit by a soft orange glow, is one of the monsters.

Waiting for us.

Chapter Twenty-One

We are so close to the next door. The only chance we have is to get inside as quickly as possible and hope it doesn't follow us.

"Go," I mouth.

Silently legging it is kind of impossible. The door is thankfully unlocked, but as it opens, the bottom scratches against the floor creating an unholy screech.

We barrel through as a replying rattle sounds and lock the door behind us. Next to us in a little kitchen area are some tables and chairs, which we barricade the door with. We duck down by the fridge and snack machine, hoping we are out of sight. The creature rattles the door and runs one of its long legs down the door. I hold my breath, and we hear it scuttle away, back down the stairs hopefully.

"I hate those things," hisses Stevie, helping me to my feet.

"Come on, we're nearly there. The sooner we get what we're looking for, the sooner we can leave."

The next room is filled with stacks of books, as you might expect. It's dark, only the security lights illuminating the floor. We pass a stack of orange trays at the end of a conveyer belt, which disappears off into the ceiling. It must take the books from down here to the people who need them upstairs.

"I think we're here."

I stop in front of a row of white rectangles sandwiched together. One of them is marked with the stack number from the Ghost Queen, but the bookshelf is sandwiched between the others. That's when I see the handle, which I crank, and slowly the stack we need and the next one separate, getting further apart with each turn.

"Woahhh," whispers Dara, running down the gap of the bookshelves.

When the gap is big enough for all three of us to easily walk down, I follow Dara in, looking for the next numbers on the Ghost Queen's list.

I find the shelf, and there, wedged between some

really big old hardbacks, is the pamphlet we were looking for.

I very gently remove it, and we take it back towards the conveyer belts where the light is better.

It's a weird little paper pamphlet, almost like an exercise book from school, but the date on the back says it is over one hundred years old.

"*The Great Plagues of Britain*, by Edwin Stroud," I read out loud.

"Come on, we've got the book. Let's go?" asks Stevie.

"We can't take it!" I hiss in horror. "This is a *library*."

"We can bring it back, probably."

"I'm with Vivi," says Dara. "We shouldn't take it. Someone else could need it."

"Urgh, you goody two-shoes," she sighs, slumping against the conveyer belt. "Well go on, open it."

I lay it flat in the tray, and take my tablet out of my bag, handing it over to Dara to take photos for us and the Ghost Queen.

"This publication serves to document the true nature of the plague of beasts that originate from the time of Lludd," I read slowly. The words are old, and formal, and it makes me tired brain hurt to pay attention to them.

219

"Clod?" says Dara, trying to pronounce the Welsh *ll*.

I skim through the words, which seem to be talking about an old story about two kings I vaguely recognise, and how the Edwin the author has evidence that it really happened, supposedly. Not that I could tell from all his waffling.

But then I turn the page.

There, drawn on the page as vivid as the one in the stairwell, is our monster. Its red eyes are stark white circles in the middle of all its darkness.

"Oh my god," whispers Stevie. "That's it."

Dara snaps pictures of the pages, as I read out the name of the beast.

"Coraniaid."

It sounds kind of beautiful. It shouldn't be the name of something so terrifying. It shouldn't be the name of something that steals children.

"It says they have . . ." I gulp, "very powerful hearing and are able to hear all sounds carried by the wind."

"Oh great," groans Stevie. "You two are the least quiet people I've ever met in my life. This is like your perfect opposite."

Dara drops their voice to a whisper. "That means . . . it could hear us now."

We look at each other for a few seconds, then hurriedly snap photos of all the remaining pages.

"There's a lift down there," whispers Stevie. "I think it'll be quieter than us trying to walk up the stairs."

I put the pamphlet back safely in the right place, and Dara cranks the bookcases together. Except when it closes, it makes the world's loudest screech, metal on metal.

Dara leaps back from the crank, and we race to the lift together.

I press the button, and that's when a familiar black shape creeps into the corner of my sight.

Maybe it was always there. It's in the top corner of the room, crouched like a spider making a web. Right over where we were standing only moments before.

I realise with horror that maybe it's playing with us.

The lift arrives, and we pelt in.

Stevie hammers at the close-the-doors button, willing the lift to go.

"Come on! Come on!!"

From my spot in the corner, I can see the cora-niaid slide down to the floor. It saunters towards us, unhurried. It knows that there's only so many places we can go, and that we're alone here.

I can't tear my eyes away from its own bright red ones.

The door pings to close, and we melt with relief. Except, that's when I notice the buttons at the bottom are illuminated, and we're going down.

"We need to go up!" cries Dara, hammering the buttons for the ground floor.

"I panicked!" says Stevie, breathless. "Do you think it understands how lifts work?"

"Oh, I sure hope not," mutters Dara.

The lift stops at the bottom-most floor, and I put my fingers over my lips as the doors open.

It's an empty floor, very quiet and darkly lit. It smells dank, like people don't come down here very often. We all hold our breath.

The lift pings, and the doors start to close, ready to take us up.

But just as the doors are about to meet, I see a flash of black.

"Oh no," I gasp.

Doors closed, the lift moves upwards, but a bang sounds above us. The lift shudders downwards suddenly, and we grab onto each other so we don't fall.

"It's on top of the lift," hisses Stevie.

Our terrified faces reflect back at us in the metal of the lift.

"I hope it can't get in," I whisper.

"The ceiling hatch. They always come through the ceiling hatch," whispers Dara, and our eyes lock on the outlined square above us, waiting for it to lift away.

But it doesn't move even though it could so easily get us. I can hear my heartbeat in my ears.

"It's messing with us," whispers Stevie. "When we reach the ground floor, everyone run."

"Shouldn't we fight it?" asks Dara, purple glowing in their hand.

"There's something weird about this one," I say. I feel like a coward, but I really want to get out of here as fast as possible.

"Not if we can help it," Stevie says.

"How are we going to get out without Gelert?"

Before we can plan, the lift stops.

"Just run for the doors," Stevie commands.

Ding

The doors open and we race forward, past the

column of books and down towards the glass doors at the front.

Stevie pulls ahead, her dark hair whipping past us.

She yanks at the doors, but they're fully locked.

Dara reaches them, and tries to spark them open, but the sparks recoils, bouncing off the metal. Stevie leaps out of the way just in time, but lands hard on her leg with a shriek.

"It's a deadbolt," they cry. They kneel to look closer at the lock, scrabbling with their awl.

We're trapped.

And that's when it catches up to us.

I'm not sure I'll ever get over the way they look. Just so clearly not of our world, especially the scribbling black of its body, a void that glitches and warps right before me. This one smells of metal and ash and burnt wires. It's been waiting for us to tire ourselves out or hurt ourselves so it can swoop in, and that's exactly what happened.

I pull Excalibur from my bag, and deeply regret that Stevie and I haven't had time for a lesson.

"Hold it in your right hand, don't grip too hard! Stand side on to it!" she shouts at me from the floor, where she crouches rubbing her swollen ankle.

I refuse to let it take another of us.

I have to protect Dara and Stevie.

And that's when Gelert appears, leaping right onto the coraniaid's back. He grabs a chunk of it in his mouth, and tears. The monster howls, distracted by the creature on top of it, and that's my opening.

Heat buzzes through my body and I charge forward, sword raised above my head. I hear a scream and realise it's *me*.

I have to protect them.

The coraniaid swings and launches Gelert off it's back. He flies across the foyer, landing hard, but just about on four feet.

And just as it turns back to face me, I jump, swinging Excalibur down with all my might.

My sword sinks deep into its chest, and for a moment, we are eye to eye as I cling on.

I wonder, just for a second, what would happen if it disappeared with me now. If it took me to where Chia is. But I'm not afraid any more. If it takes me, I'll fight with all my might to escape.

But it doesn't take me anywhere.

It explodes into a cloud of ash.

I bend over, gasping for my breath. I can't get

enough air and my skin is crawling and everything feels electric.

But then Gelert is there, licking my face. Licking my tears. The fire inside me dulls, and I throw my arms around him, careful not to catch him with the sword. I nuzzle my face into his thick wiry hair, breathing in his fresh grass and doggy scent.

I know what that feeling was. I'm close to a meltdown. It's the point when my autistic brain can't cope any more. I've not had time to process any of the life-changing or nightmarish events from the last few days, and it threatens to spill out of me. But we're not safe yet, and I have to hold on.

A large clunk sounds, and Dara is through one of the doors. To my relief, no alarms go off either – they must have taken them out already.

"Let's go," Stevie says, as Dara pulls her to her feet. I hear them whisper, "I've got you."

I honestly can't remember the walk back to the portal to the Unlands. We pause here to catch our breath, but this where I really start to feel bad. All the energy in me is gone, and instead I'm drowning, slowly.

It feels like seconds before Stevie tells us we have

to go.

"I can't. Too tired," I whisper.

"Get up," she snaps, clearly in pain herself. "You have to push through this."

"Don't," I moan. "I can't."

My teeth ache, and I realise that the good Gelert did in calming me down has been undone. Everything from the last few weeks has built up inside my head like a thick pressure, and now it feels like it's all going to spill out.

"You can. You have to."

"Stevie," Dara warns, scooting over to me. "Go easy on her."

"Pushing through that discomfort is important and the basis of any athletic training," she says haughtily, as though her twisted ankle is comparable to what I know is happening to me.

I don't know why, but this seems to be what tips me over the edge.

"This isn't sports," I snap, as the drowning morphs to something hotter. "And I've had enough of neurotypical people telling me what I'm experiencing isn't right or real, so you can bog off with that."

My words echo inside my own skull.

"Come on, I don't think she meant it that way either, Vivi," pleads Dara.

"Are you both actually kidding me?" Stevie snaps. "I'm the one with zero powers and I'm taking all this so much more seriously than either of you."

"That's not true," pleads Dara. "We're all just tired."

"So what? Tiredness. Pain. You can push through it. You have to learn to push through that. This isn't fun and games. Chia's life could be at stake!"

This is all too much. Too much pressure, too much responsibility.

Oh, Vivi that's not really how it is. You can't be feeling that way. Just listen to us, we're right. We tell the truth. That's what Kelly and the others used to say. It's only a matter of time before Dara and Stevie see what the others saw in me, the thing that the others hated. Dara's sticking up for me now, but soon they'll be tired of being in the middle, of accommodating me.

My head is full of bees or fire or something truly horrible that cannot be contained and is absolutely going to explode everywhere if everyone doesn't shut up.

"Ste, just because being yelled at works for you, doesn't mean it works for us," Dara tries again.

"Come on, let's not argue. We need to get home."

"Oh, so it's my fault now? I volunteered to help you, I put myself in danger and now you're critiquing the way I coach you?"

"And we're grateful for your help, but not if it makes things worse for us. This isn't helping Vivi, or me. And I know you're scared—"

"Someone has to be!! Chia is gone! And I have to push you, because one day you two are going to face some nightmare creature that's going to seriously hurt you, and I'm not going to be able to help you. So yes, I am going to push you hard now, because I have to."

That's when I realise that a meltdown really is coming now. Like a boulder running down a slope, it can't be stopped.

"Guys," I bleat, tears spilling down my cheeks. They can't hear me. Their yells blur into a wall of sound.

Everything is a hyper-speed blur of terrible. My feet tangle in themselves as I stand up and try to get away.

I run. It's the only thing that my body knows how to do. My feet pound and I have no idea where I am, but if I stop . . .

Something hits me in the head, and I drop to my knees. Blood comes away on my hand as I wipe my forehead.

And I realise I'm in the Unlands. I've run *into* the Unlands, and straight into one of the crystals.

There's a monster running right at me, and I have nothing left. I can't yell or fight. This is it.

But then the monster is flung out the way, like it's been hit by a moving vehicle. It collides with the wall in a sickening crack and disappears. It happens so fast.

This seems to be the last thing I can process, because then the explosion happens. All I can see is white, and hot fire races all over me. I'm crying, maybe screaming? Something hits me in the head again, and I'm pretty sure that it was me this time. I drop back to my knees.

And then, almost as quickly as it started, the colour seeps back in. The fury becomes a dull emptiness. Beside me, I sense Gelert, and I reach out to him. His licks the blood from my forehead.

"Stars, Vivi. Are you okay?" asks Dara, panting.

"Give her some space," says Stevie. "Let her breathe."

Their voices are muffled. My head feels stuffed

with cotton wool, which is not surprising since both me and a crystal decided to attack it.

I'm mortified. I put us in danger, and there was a monster. I could have killed us. But before the shame can take over me, I hear something strange.

The sound of hooves.

I look up and there, finally, inexplicably, is Chia riding a white horse.

"Found you!" she cries, slipping off the horse's back. "Finally!"

Stevie collides with Chia, all tears and shrieks of joy. Dara joins them, but everyone is speaking over each other, and it blurs into one big sound.

Chia pats the horse's great neck. "This is Eirlys. Eirlys, this is the gang."

I'm still dazed so everything is in soft focus, apart from the truly enormous horse.

Gelert helps me to my feet, and when Chia comes to me, she doesn't touch me. I guess she figured out I had a meltdown.

Eirlys approaches, and huffs a hot, straw-scented breath all over me. It's a nice *hello*. Her mane is glimmering starlight, and her fur foggy. I know normal horses are big, but Eirlys is really, *really* big.

"Why is the neighbour's dog here?" she asks.

"I don't belong to anyone," he huffs, and I expect her to shriek or cry out or anything, but she just nods. I mean, it's probably not even the weirdest thing she's seen today.

"Do you know the way out?" she asks us all, and Stevie explains the way.

"I think Eirlys can take us back, right?" Chia asks the horse.

The horse nods her great head and does a big huff in agreement. Misty steps up to her back appear in the air, which Chia walks up, and sits on Eirlys' back. She holds out a hand to us.

"Come on. It's safe."

Too exhausted to question anything, we clamber up onto the horse – Chia in front, Stevie and I in the middle, and Dara at the end, holding tightly to me. I worry briefly about whether the four of us are too heavy for a horse, but then, as Gelert would say, I should probably stop thinking magical things act like normal stuff from our world.

Eirlys trots through the caverns, easily navigating the twists and turns, even when the tunnels narrow so all four of us have to duck.

I'm nauseous from my meltdown, but one thought keeps repeating in my mind. Was Chia looking for us? Did she rescue me? Did she kill that monster? Could she be the next calon? It's been solidly windy in London for the last week, but I hadn't thought about if that was weird because I've only just moved here. For all I know, London is a really windy city . . . but something in my gut tells me that's not true.

Within what feels like seconds, we reach the usual portal. And in a rush, we're through, and dismounting the horse one by one. Eirlys nuzzles Chia's face, and disappears back through to the Unlands, leaving behind her a cloud of mist.

That's when I notice it. Slung around her neck, threaded through her necklace, is a horseshoe, sparkling silver in the crystal light.

I see the realisation pass over Gelert first, then Dara and finally Stevie, who goes rigid. "It's you," she whispers, holding her voice steady, but I can hear the tiniest, tiniest crack of pain in there. "It's you." There's a gap where 'not me' should be, hanging in the air.

"What's me?" Chia asks, holding the necklace out. No one says anything, so she drops it back down against her skin, and I swear it glows, like a shooting star. To my relief, she says, "Look, I think we should focus on getting home before you drop whatever it is you want to tell me. I've . . . kind of had a weird few days, or week, or however long it's been."

I have nothing left in me. "Take me home Gelert," I whisper.

And he does.

Chapter Twenty-Two

Meltdowns is warp time. Not in a cool magical power kind of way. It's a blurry nothing. I feel like the slowly growing sludgy mess at the side of the road that happens when it snows.

Gelert takes me right to my bedroom, and I lie down on my bed without swapping into pyjamas. As my body sinks into the mattress, Gelert hops up and lies down across my legs. We breathe in sync. I put on some rain sounds to calm us both.

"Thank you," I whisper. I reach down and rub the muscly gap between his shoulder blades, but he winces.

I turn the light on and get off the bed. He licks at one of his front legs, and I realise he's got a gnarly cut down it. It's not deep, but it must have been where the coraniaid threw him.

Our first aid kit lives under the sink in the bathroom, so I go to get it, even though the dog first aid pages on the internet seem to think most things aren't dog safe. Gelert might be a ghost, but I still want to be careful with him.

In the mirror, I see the cut on my forehead is surrounded by purple bruise. Hopefully I can convince the Mums that I fell out of bed, because they're definitely going to have questions.

I soak a mostly clean flannel in warm water and take it back with me.

"This might sting," I say, as I press it against him.

To his credit, he hardly bares his teeth at all. I dress his leg so it can stay clean . . . if he even gets dirty. I don't know how I'd explain an infection on my thousand-year-old ghost dogs leg to a vet.

I tuck a blanket round us both, and soon we're both asleep.

Mumma wakes me up sometime later – luckily Gelert seems to have vanished – and the falling out of bed story is immediately met with a raised eyebrow. They know exactly how I look after a meltdown: wrung out. She lets me go back to sleep, instead of going to school.

Around lunch time, I get back up and go downstairs.

Mam is home, which is weird. She holds her arms out to me, and I slide onto her lap. She kisses the Baby Yoda plaster on my forehead.

"Do you want to tell us what's being going on?" Mam's voice is soft but serious, the particular tone that always comes out when we talk about meltdowns.

I hate lying, and I'm bad at it, but also I don't think they'd believe me if I told them we were in the British Library's basements being chased by monsters.

"Nothing. I'm just tired." They glance at each other. "What?"

"Baban, I just think maybe you've been pushing it a bit hard," begins Mam. "You've joined a new school and moved to a new place, and we're really glad you've got some new friends, but you don't know them very well yet."

Mumma taps her fingers against her mug, her wedding ring clanging off the ceramic. "We just think maybe you should take some time out from the play and everything. Just for a bit?"

I suppress a laugh as I remember they still think I'm a budding actor. The truth is so much more complicated.

"Why are you home?" I ask Mam.

"Just wanted to be nearby, just in case." She gives me a brave smile. They must be so worried about me. I think it must be hard being a parent to someone who finds the regular world so hard at the best of times, knowing there's only so much you can do.

I give her a kiss on the cheek.

"Do you want to go back to bed for the rest of the day?" Mumma says.

I nod and give her one too.

As I take the stairs two at a time, I hear Mam say, "I don't know how we're going to make this okay for her."

Part of me thinks that maybe this is my way out. *Sorry guys, I can't help save the world, I'm grounded for my own good.* If only it was that simple.

Back in bed I burrow into the covers, determined to never come out again. Something tickles my foot, and I'm so tired I don't even flinch. If there's a monster in my bed after everything, I'm going to be so angry.

Luckily, it's just one very large dog reappearing. He stretches out next to me, and I get a whiff of something very doggy.

"Are you wet, as well? Could you perhaps not use my bed as a towel?"

"It's only a bit of water, mun. I thought you'd be used to that by now. Why are you still here anyway? I normally have the bed to myself in the day."

"No wonder my bed smells weird now," I huff. "I'm off sick. And the Mums said I'm not allowed to do the play any more so I dunno, I guess all this is over."

"Don't be dramatic."

"Don't be dramatic says a ghost dog that regularly likes to leap out of my wardrobe or appear suddenly in front of strangers? You love the drama."

He doesn't reply for a moment, and surprises me a little when he asks, "What was it, that thing that happened to you?"

"A meltdown," I whisper.

"It looked pretty rubbish." He lays his head on my chest, big watery eyes staring right at me. I rub the tips of his remarkably soft ears with my fingers.

"It felt rubbish. Like being a shaken up fizzy pop bottle."

"I don't know what that is."

"A volcano?"

"Mmm."

My turn to roll my eyes. "It's like an explosion. Hang on, I thought you could read? What have you been doing the last 1000 years other than not learning about fizzy pop, volcanoes and autism?"

He huffs. "Waiting around for—"

"Yeah yeah, I get it." I bite my bottom lip. "God, this is all so much."

"What is?"

"Being hurt by people."

"Did they hurt you?"

"No, but . . . Not directly. They just don't understand me, I don't think. I'm worried . . . What if they see it . . ."

"See what?"

"All the things about me that make me different from them, and what if they start to hate it like . . . like everyone else did."

A low growl sounds from Gelert's chest. "Like who?"

I'm so taken aback by this sudden anger on my behalf that it takes me a minute to remember I've not told him or the others about this.

"At my old school, I had friends. Or at least, they acted like they were for a while." I take a deep breath. "But then they realised that they could be mean to me, and I'd not really understand it if they were nice to me again after. Because they were my *friends*, I just thought it was part of friendship, that sometimes they do things that upset you, or hurt you. Like, I knew about falling out with someone, but no one told me friends weren't supposed to pick on you. That's one of the hard things about being autistic – I don't always understand why people do some things."

Gelert growls again. "What in the flip?! I'm no expert on human children, but no one should make you feel like that."

"I know that *now*," I say, feeling the urge to defend my past self. "But it was only when one of them hurt me and someone saw and told my teacher that I found out it wasn't supposed to be like that. It was so *horrible*. When I asked them to stop being mean to me, they would for like a day, and then it'd start again. Even when the teacher said they had to stop bullying me, they'd wait until no one was watching . . ."

I trail off but Gelert waits quietly for me to keep going.

"It's hard to trust new people because what if they do the same thing? What if I don't notice it happening? Or maybe I was wrong, and they didn't like me at all," I say, wiping my tears. "What if Dara, Stevie and Chia feel stuck with me? Maybe I'm the problem. Maybe I'm just *broken*."

Gelert sits up suddenly, grabbing my plaid jacket that was hanging on the back of my chair with his teeth. He flings it at me.

"Put this on, and then hold onto me, right?"

Exhausted, I just do as he says. I shuck the jacket on and wrap my arms around his neck, unsure what is about to happen.

In a flash, we move. We are definitely not in my bedroom anymore. Rushing wind in a sea of nothingness. The smell of burning metal. Glaring white. It's all over in a matter of seconds

And then we're in a field.

Not just any field, but a wide expanse of field bordered by mountains and a rushing stream somewhere to my left. It's all strangely familiar. The air tastes right – mulch and greenery and sheep. The cold air mists with drizzle and fuzzes in my chest. It's chilly enough that I'm glad Gelert made me put on a jacket.

"Where are we?"

"Somewhere important."

My feet feel cold, and I look down to discover I'm still wearing my fuzzy bed socks. "Uh oh," I say uselessly. They feel disgusting as they soak up all the moisture.

Gelert leads me down a path that cuts through the

field. Either the sheep are too busy grazing to care or they can't see him, but they don't react at all, even when we get close. One ewe is nestled into a ledge on a stone wall, chewing happily.

"*Why* are we here?" I press.

"I wanted to tell you a story about trust," he says, turning a corner into a new field. Ahead of us are two trees, ringed by a low fence.

Quietly, he adds, "I am going to tell you the story of how I died."

Obviously, I know he's a ghost.

But, somehow, it hadn't connected in my head that this meant he *died* at some point. I just thought of him as immortal, rather than somewhere between alive and dead.

"I used to be a hunting dog. A very good one, in fact," he begins. "And I used to belong to a King named Llewelyn."

"Are we talking like Buckingham Palace royalty?" No wonder he always acted like he owned the place. At one point he probably did. Or his owner did.

"No, no. Plus, Buckingham Palace didn't exist a thousand years ago. There used to be a lot more Kings then. Kings of smaller bits of the country."

"Where was he King of?"

"Here. What you know as North Wales—"

"We're home?" I cry, interrupting him. I spin round, letting the cloudy silver skies meld with the green mountains and distant piles of slate. My heart aches with hiraeth. And then I remember why I'm here. "Sorry, I've just missed Wales a lot. Please continue."

"Right here, where we are standing, there was Llewelyn's hunting lodge. I lived here, and when he visited, we'd go hunting up into Eryrri."

"What did you hunt?"

"Boar. Deer. Other things."

I'm quietly impressed. We walk on. Ahead, under the trees, I see two large grey stones.

"On the occasion of our last meeting, he brought with him the new Prince. He was a funny little creature, all pink and wailing, noisy as anything. Would only calm down if I was there, you know. Slept like a log if I was on guard. And the Queen had died, stars rest her, so anything that made the babe happy pleased the King too. One night, Llewelyn was called away, and though he didn't want to go, he told me to watch over the baby."

As he talks, I become more and more aware of

how wet my sodden socks are. It's hard to concentrate, so I slip them off, wincing at the cold.

"That night, I sensed something in the room with us. A wolf."

I expect the sheep to shrink back at the word wolf, but they just continue chewing.

"Wolves had been bothering the farmers down the valley. And this was the biggest wolf I'd seen in years, grown strong on all those sheep. Muscles like no other, and it wanted the little Prince."

"I thought wolves didn't hurt people," I whisper.

"Not always, but times were different then. Wolves were different then. Wilder. Sometimes they came with a spark of magic that made them even more dangerous."

"What happened?" I ask, as we stop under the trees. Mist turns to drizzle, and I'm glad for the shelter.

"I defended that baby with my life. It was a challenge, but I was young and fit." He says this with pride.

"The wolf didn't kill you?"

"No."

"So, what did?"

He inclines his head towards the stones, which

are pretty big. And they're not just rocks. They're covered in words. One in Welsh, and one in English.

At the top of the Welsh one it says "Bedd Gelert", and the other . . . "Gelert's grave."

A shriek escapes me before I can hold it back.

"Calm yourself, will you?" he says.

"Sorry, this is just . . . kind of eerie. You know, talking to you, while we're looking at your grave."

He sniffs at the engraved stones, and I wonder if he really is buried here.

"Wait . . . does that mean we're in Beddgelert? And that they named the whole town after your grave?"

"Correct on both counts."

"Man . . . that's kind of weird isn't it? I'm sorry?" I'm not sure if I'm supposed to comfort him about this, but it is super weird. I would not love it if someone named a village 'Vivisgrave'.

"What happened after that?"

"Well, I killed the wolf, didn't I? Useless thing had knocked the cot over, but the babe was alright, all wrapped up in his blankets. He seemed safe and I didn't want to move him given all the blood. So, I just lay with him, he calmed down, and we both fell asleep. And that's the last thing I remember."

"You died in your sleep?"

"I was *killed*." After a deep sigh, he says, "By the King."

A stone drops in my stomach. "No," I whisper. "But you didn't hurt the Prince. You saved him!"

"You know that. I know that. But if you walk into your baby's room and find it covered in blood, cot overturned, no crying . . . What are you going to do? Put two and two together, and get seven, like he did."

"And he killed you for it."

"He did." Gelert says it so simply, like it doesn't tear him up inside. I don't understand. I feel water running down my cheeks but it's not rain breaking through the leaves; I'm crying.

"Now, listen to me girl," he says, nudging my hand with his long-bearded snout. "I know you were hurt by your so-called friends in your old school."

I gulp, trying to dislodge the painful lump in my throat.

"It's not your fault that happened. It doesn't mean there's something wrong with you. People are capable of doing terrible things to each other, for reasons that usually only make any sense to them."

Mam used to say they were jealous, I think. Not

247

that I could see why.

"But Dara and Stevie are not the same people who hurt you. I know they frightened you with all that bickering, but they care about you, right? Chia too, I expect. She did save you with a blinking great horse."

We laugh quietly together.

"Ignore all this magic stuff for a second. If you hold yourself back from them, and their friendship, the bullies keep winning, don't they? They're still holding power over you, making you smaller than you deserve to be. Put yourself and your future happiness first."

"I'm scared," I whisper finally.

"Of course, you're scared. You think I wasn't scared? Tucking down next to you with that sword under your bed?"

My stomach swoops. "Oh Gel."

"But you're not Llewellyn, and I had to choose to trust you or else I wouldn't know you, annoying as you are."

He's right. I throw my arms around him. His thick silver fur is heavy with mist-water. He leans hard against me. "I promise, I will never ever hurt you like that."

"Luckily you can't kill a dog that's already dead."

"I mean it," I say, squeezing him. "I'll be with you for

all my life, if you want me. You don't have to be alone again. I know how sad and scary it can be to feel like you have no one, but you have me."

His thick tail wags slowly against the floor, tapping against my thigh.

"Hmmm. You're very annoying though. What if I decide I've had enough?" he says, and for a moment I think he's being serious.

"Bog off," I laugh, playfully pushing him off.

He nudges me back with his big head.

"Is this why you don't stay with us all the time? Why you're always disappearing?"

"I didn't say it was an immediate fix," he says softly. "It'll be something I have to work through for a long time – you too no doubt – but that doesn't mean it's not worth it." He says the last bit quietly, like he's embarrassed to say it out loud.

"You're right," I sigh.

We stay there, my arms wrapped around his great body, learning to trust each other as the rain falls around us. He is right. I don't want to be small any more. I want to be me, and liked for who I am. And I think Dara, Stevie and Chia might be the right friends for me. If I let them be.

Chapter Twenty-Three

Despite Gelert's pep talk, I still dread going back to school. I insist on going back the next day, even though the Mums are really not sure about it, and hover around me like I'm going to fall apart.

When I get to the library, Stevie and Dara are already there. They leap up as I arrive.

"Hi," Dara says nervously. "Are you okay?"

I take a deep breath. "I am now. But we should probably talk."

We flop down into our usual chairs, pointedly not looking at each other as we wait for someone else to start.

"Okay, I'll start. I'm sorry," begins Stevie. "I got caught up in doing what I thought was the right thing, and I didn't stop to think that maybe I could change that, adapt to what worked for you both. That's what a good coach should do, and I'm sorry about that."

"You were scared, for us and Chia," I say. "And hurt. Is your ankle okay?"

She nods. "But that's not an excuse. If I had listened, or calmed myself down, maybe you wouldn't have gotten so upset, and hurt. I'll listen better, from now on."

"Thank you," I say. "I probably should have told you about meltdowns. It's not your fault you didn't realise what was happening, and . . . I've been trying to keep you both at arm's length. I know I haven't been the easiest to have around, and there's something I should probably tell you that explains it."

"You can tell us," says Dara.

And so, I tell them everything I told Gelert, and how it made me scared of making friends again. It feels so trivial compared to us fighting literal monsters, and part of me still expects them to shrug it off. But when I look up, Stevie's eyes are lit by flames, and Dara's face is creased with worry.

"Oh my god. I will fight them," she spits out. "I will actually fight these people. Right now! How

251

dare they!!"

"I'm right there with you," says Dara, looking more quietly furious than I've ever seen them. "Vivi, I'm so sorry that you were dealing with this on top of everything else."

"What scumbags! What horrible bullies!" Stevie mutters what I'm pretty sure are curses under her breath.

"Yeah, I was kind of planning on not making any friends and just getting through the next few years without anyone noticing," I mumble. "That didn't quite work out."

"Oh god, and you ended up getting forced together with Dara of all people," laughs Stevie.

"And you! Miss *I'm going to coach you and save you from being useless tadpoles*," says Dara, mimicking Stevie's voice.

"I didn't call you tadpoles," she says. "I probably should though."

We all laugh, and it feels right.

"So yeah, I've not really been . . . all in, I guess. Not really. So, you weren't wrong Stevie, I wasn't taking it seriously because I was too busy being scared of getting close to you both."

"I still could have gone about it in a nicer way," she admits. "Nice isn't my default, but I'll work on it."

"That's okay," I say. "I kind of like that I always know how you're really feeling. And if you want, I'll tell you some more autism stuff, so you know what it looks like when I'm not okay."

"Please," Stevie says, and Dara nods.

"You know, the weirdest thing about all this is that Gelert gave me the pep talk about friendship."

At the mention of his name, Gelert appears, settling himself down by my feet.

"I don't think I'll ever get used to that," sighs Stevie. "Also . . . I . . . I thought it was going to be me. That I'd be the next calon."

"We did too," I admit.

"That kind of makes me feel better about it. I mean, I'm already part of it all, so you'd think the universe would just be like may as well be her and give me some actual powers so I can be useful." Her mouth is a snarl, like she really wants to kick something out of frustration.

"Stevie, come on. You're an important part of the team. Our team," Dara says.

"That's easy for you to say, sparky."

"You literally saved me in the Science Museum," I add. I don't know what to say to comfort her, but the gap of when I'm supposed to say something is closing, and I panic when what comes out of my mouth is, "but we can't change that it's Chia."

I've swung too far the wrong way; said something harsh when I was trying to work out what she would want to hear. Hot panic rushes through my body, threatening to become a blazing inferno for, once again, saying the wrong thing.

But to my relief, Stevie takes a deep breath and nods. The panic pauses, my heart slowing down. "Vivi's right. I can be sad about it, but that doesn't change the situation. And a good coach doesn't let that get in the way of her job. Thanks, Vivi."

All the anxiety ebbs away, like someone uncorked me.

"Wow, it's emotion-central in here," says Chia, strides in, closing the door behind her. She starts to speak but trails off as she sees Gelert. "Is he allowed to be here?"

"I go where I like," he murmurs.

Turns out Chia had taken the day off too, and had also spent it mostly asleep. I ask what things have been like at home since she got back. She slumps down in the last remaining chair.

"That's the weirdest thing about all this . . . well, not the *weirdest* but definitely strange. Mummy didn't bat an eye. As far as she and my stepdad Cameron were concerned, I'd not been gone. The only person who had noticed I was gone was Ife. She was really freaked out."

"Weird," Dara says.

I shiver. If they can forget us temporarily, does that mean they could forget us for good?

"The thing I can't get over," she says slowly. "Is that I to you guys I was gone for four days. It felt double that, at least. I don't really know how I lasted that long."

"Time moves faster in the Unlands," says Dara. "We checked when we went to the library. I timed it."

"When Vivi and I were there after the Science Museum it felt so long, but out here it was barely half a day. Everything felt off," says Stevie.

"Where did the coraniaid take you?" I ask.

"You know, I'm weirdly glad those things have a name," she says with a shiver. "It . . . They put me in a room with a bunch of other kids. Like, a bunch of us. Maybe less than ten? They kept moving us around and everyone was so scared, so it was hard to keep track of everyone."

"Do you remember any of their names?"

"Yeah, there was this tall red-haired girl called Isabella who had teamed up with Clare, who was super quiet and frightened. She wouldn't let anyone go near her. And then there was a boy called Simon, I think? I know it seems weird that I don't know everyone's names, but it was like I *couldn't* remember? None of us could. I don't know . . . Everyone was about our age, which is strange when you think about it."

I glance at the others. We have so much to tell her. But Clare was one of the names from the Ghost Queen's posts, so at least we know where she's gone.

"On the third day, we staged an escape. There were less of the monsters around, so we basically all ran off in other directions."

"The morning we were at the Science Museum," Dara says, doing the maths.

"But there was only one there," I say. "I was fighting it."

Dara quietly shakes their head. "It wasn't the only one."

My stomach plummets. I thought I'd been keeping the one dangerous monster at bay while everyone could escape, and that wasn't even true. I want to ask them more, but Chia keeps going.

"I got split up from the others almost immediately and ended up just wandering around on my own, marking the tunnels with little squares so I knew where I'd been," Chia continues. "But I started feeling this weird sensation, like I was being pulled to something."

As she speaks, she unclips the horseshoe from her necklace. When she places it in her palm, it grows back to the size of a normal horseshoe, but it glows in her palm. It's slim and light and looks almost like a discus.

"I found this in the dirt, and when I touched it, I felt so, so strange. But in a good way. And then suddenly there was one of those monsters there, and I screamed at it . . . and it blew down the tunnel."

We're quiet as Gelert walks over to Chia, sniffing up and down her body. She giggles, scratching his forehead.

"You rode a white horse?" he asks and Chia nods. "You must be Rhiannon. Welcome." I almost expect he's going to launch into the story of who Rhiannon is, but Dara beats him to it, instead launching into The Talk. Who we are, and why this is happening. What we think the coraniaids wanted: us, the calonnau. And all the stuff that has yet to happen.

This is the second time I've heard The Talk, but this time I get to watch, and I can see how much it takes out of Dara. It must've been really hard the first time. At least now they have Stevie and I to chip in.

Chia nods along from the ratty armchair, taking it all in. Gelert lays his head in her lap, and she strokes his ears. No wonder he's nice to her.

Finding the third calon means we're halfway to finding everyone we need to stop Arawn.

But we have no leads on who they could be. Dara was alone for months before they found me. And Chia went through so much. I can't help but worry about what we might face to find the next three calonnau.

"Are you alright?" I ask Chia when Dara's done.

Chia laughs. "I mean, no. But . . . this kind of makes sense. And at least I know that I've got you guys along with me; that's much better than roaming around the Unlands alone." She's quiet for a moment, and it's clear she has more to say. But the moment passes, and instead she smiles. "It's a pretty cool talisman at least. I wonder what it can do."

"You lucked out. Dara just got some weird pokey thing," laughs Stevie.

"It's an awl!" they huff.

"And Vivi got a sword she can't use. Useless."

"I used it once really well," I sniff.

"Sure. But you've got some fencing lessons in your future."

I groan, and everyone laughs.

"So, who is Rhiannon. Or was? Is?" asks Chia.

"It's kind of both," I sigh.

Head still in her lap, Gelert softly growls. "I only remember the horse." Poor Gelert. He'd remembered so much about Nimuë and Ceridwen that I think all of us were hoping his memories would restore as soon as we found someone, but I guess it's more complicated than that.

"That's okay, friend," she says, scratching under his chin. His tail softly wags.

"I'll ask Nimuë," I say. "I can remember Rhiannon a bit from one of Mumma's books. She's always drawn with the moon too, as well as the horse."

"So, Chia's like some goth horse girl?" snorts Stevie,

259

and Chia laughs as well.

"I've never even had a riding lesson before," she laughs. "I mean . . . it was kind of easy though. Like we were in sync. I hope I get to see her again."

"I hope I never have to ride a horse again," says Stevie. "Once was quite enough."

"Don't be mean about my horse or I'll blow you over," Chia hisses.

"Water, electricity, and now wind," I say. "I wonder if all the powers are elemental."

"Do you feel like showing us what you can do?" Dara asks, and Chia nods eagerly.

Stevie kneels next to the chair Chia sits in, and turns Chia's hand over, so her palm faces up. "Think about how you felt in the Unlands. When you saw us in the Unlands, exhausted and half-dead and running, and how that monster was running at us. How did it make you feel?"

Chia gulps as the feelings rush back to her. She closes her eyes, and begins to hum, a melody I don't recognise. It's beautiful, full of the control and confidence I heard when she sang.

In the centre of her palm white, misty air gathers, forming a perfect miniature tornado. It moves as she hums. She opens her eyes slowly, gasping at the power in her hand. It snuffs out as she closes her palm.

"Okay," Chia says, taking it all in. "But there better not be any 'Chia's got wind' jokes, alright?"

"I definitely can't promise that," admits Dara.

"So, you're electricity then. Stevie's always complaining that you give her static shocks," she laughs at Dara, whose ears turn pink.

"Mine's water, which is useful as long as there is water." I pull a big bottle of water out of my rucksack. "We make sure I always have some with me, just in case."

"And now, we just have to work out how to put all of this together to take out the coraniaids, now that we know what they are," says Stevie.

"Is that their name?" asks Chia and we nod. To my surprise, this time it's Stevie who launches into an explanation of the Ghost Queen and how we broke into the British Library. I catch Dara smiling with pride.

"Speaking of," I say turning to Gelert, realising I haven't had chance to ask him in all the chaos. "We found this pamphlet that talked about them being part of a plague."

"That's right, Clod!" says Dara, pronouncing it totally wrong.

"Lludd, King Lludd," I correct. "Do you have the photos?"

Their face flushes. "Yeah so, all that frying doors and cameras . . . I fried my phone too. I haven't managed to recover them yet."

"Do you know the story Gelert?" I ask.

He yawns, annoyed that he's been disturbed. "I know the one. I wasn't there, it was long before my time. So, I only know the story that got told afterwards, probably the same story in your pamphlet. Won't surprise you that it's full of artistic silliness." He sits up, looking like he's about to give us a proper lecture. "King Lludd was a King of Britain, and early into his rule there were three plagues. There was a horrible scream that kept everyone up: that was actually two dragons having a scrap on the nightly. And some magician fella was putting everyone at court to sleep and stealing all their food, which is cracking, but don't worry about that one either. The important one was some creature that kept infest-ing everywhere and because they've got such good hearing, they kept overhearing all his plans to get rid of them."

"The coraniaids," I whisper. "There was a drawing next to it."

"Hmm," he sniffs. "That explains why I didn't think of them. They're usually described as tiny little coblyn type creatures."

Dara shudders. "They are definitely not coblyns. They're worse, somehow."

"Anyway, Lludd didn't know what to do, so he had to get advice from his brother, the King of France. Called him up on this long bronze horn across the English Channel."

"I'm sorry. A horn over the channel?"

He gives me a dog shrug.

"Don't say it," I mutter. *Stop expecting magical objects to behave like normal things Vivi Conway*, his smug voice says in my head.

"I wasn't going to; I think it probably is tosh. Probably just a metaphor for letters or something daft, isn't it. Anyway, he said to crush up this insect in the water supply, and it killed all the blighters."

"I guess we have no idea what this insect is," I say, and he does another sniff-shrug. If the insect came from France, there was even a chance we didn't have it here. Plus, it's not like we've ever seen them just stopping for a drink either, so I've no idea how we'd dose them. "So, we're back to square one?"

"Not quite," says Stevie. "We know what they are. Chia knows where the kids were. We just need to think strategy. Then we can go back to the Unlands and rescue the other kids."

She kicks Dara's foot gently with her own. "You're quiet."

"Just thinking."

"Inventing?" I ask, hopefully.

"Not yet, but if they can always hear us, if we can't mask our sound, we have no chance of ambushing them. It puts them at the advantage," they say. "I'm working on it."

I catch Stevie smirking with pride from the corner of my eye.

"Wait, I've got one more question," says Chia, her eyes huge and watery. "Was the play all a cover for this?"

"Oh, err, yeah. Sorry," says Dara.

"Oh man," she groans. "At least I had that to look forward to."

"You'll get your big break another day," Stevie says.

"Perhaps when I'm done being a magical horse girl," Chia laughs, and we all join in. "So, what's next?"

"Training," says Stevie, fully in coach mode. "After Science Club. I want to see where all your powers are – Dara and I did a bit yesterday – and we can plan our rescue." She falters a little and adds, "If that's good for you all?"

My heart swells a little, and even though I'm tired, with all this, all of us together, I feel ready to keep going. "I'm in," I say, holding my hand out.

We all put our hands in together, and because we hadn't pre-agreed a word, we end up shouting a jumble of what sounds like "go team" and "kick butt" and Dara just makes a loud cheering noise.

"You four are very strange indeed," says Gelert, before making a dramatic exit, just because he can.

Chapter Twenty-Four

It's so nice to have Chia back in school with us that time flies, but in a good way for once. It's nice to have a kind of normal Thursday . . . if you just forget all the other stuff that's happened.

We're all still tired from the last week of chaos, so after lunch we ask our English teacher Ms. Sutcliff if we can go do quiet study in the library. We must have been the first students to ever ask her this, as she was a mixture of delighted and surprised as she ushered us out.

Dara is quiet, which as you might expect is quite unusual for them, but every now and then I catch them scribbling something down in the corner of their notebook. The last thing I see was "ask Mr. R about stopping sounds."

Luckily, we have Science Club after school, and luckily, we're the only people who've actually turned up. Perhaps everyone else has had enough of science for one week.

Before Mr. Reynolds can start us off on whatever he had planned, Dara launches into the problem: how to manage sound design for the play I keep forgetting is our cover story.

As they speak, I worry that Mr. Reynolds might be suspicious of our sudden interest in sound, but once again his eyes light up, another teacher thrilled that we want to learn something. I make a mental note to be suddenly deeply enthusiastic about someone's class whenever I need something.

"So, if we're thinking about ways to prevent sound from reaching someone else's ears, we must think of it in two ways. How do you stop sound from being heard and how do you stop making sound? But first we need to know what is sound?"

"Isn't it like vibrations?" says Dara. "The particles in something vibrates and that makes a sound wave."

"Yeah, that's what happens when I sing. My vocal chords vibrate. See?" Chia demonstrates with a glassy sounding *ahhhhh*. "And then you lucky people get to hear it."

"That's absolutely right," he says, looking like he might explode with joy. "Sound is a kind of energy that forms when things vibrate. Sound travels through the air because particles bump together, making more vibrations, until it reaches your ear. So, when we want to disrupt sound, we need to look at ways to reduce those vibrations."

Mr. Reynolds leans back from his desk and grabs a roll of blue paper towel that's for emergency spills, setting it on the desk next to his empty and very stained coffee cup.

"When I hit my pen on something, I make a vibration." He taps his pen against his cup. A bright sound rings out. "This mug is made of a very hard substance, ceramic, so there's a lot of vibration and a nice loud sound."

Then he does the same to the roll of paper towels. There's a very tiny, muffled thump. "But this is soft, so not much vibration at all. In fact, it absorbs the vibrations."

"So, if we want to make less sound, we need lots of soft things?" I ask.

"That's right. It helps muffle the sound that's

being made."

Stevie picks up the paper towels. "Let's wrap Dara up in this and see if it makes a difference."

"Me? Why me?"

"Sometimes, I just wish I could muffle you. Like just a bit."

Dara wails.

"I vote we do Stevie!" laughs Chia.

"Changed my mind. Let's wrap up noise-maker general over here," Stevie laughs, grabbing Chia around the waist. They giggle and scuffle for a moment, while Mr Reynolds quietly puts the paper towel roll back in its place, out of reach.

"What about using other sounds to distract? Like, when I get overloaded, I can't separate out different sounds easily. Do other people get that? Would that sort of thing work on someone else?" I ask.

Mr. Reynolds thinks for a moment. "Lots of sound as a kind of sensory barrage probably would affect everyone, unless they had heavy sound blocking gear."

That idea is definitely out. I don't have enough ear defenders for all of us.

"Plus, that wouldn't be great for people attending

a play, Vivi."

"Yes! The play," I say, unconvincingly. "I was just
. . . curious. About ways sounds are used and how
it works, you know?"

'Curious' turns out to be the magic word for teachers.

"Distraction can be a good technique for other
things though. Hey, do you know that when a group
of chimpanzees hunt monkeys some of them will
make a lot of noise to distract the monkey, or scare
it towards other chimpanzees who lie in wait to
trap it."

"Yikes," says Dara.

"Poor monkeys," whispers Chia.

"Wow. That's clever," says Stevie. "An effective
teamwork strategy."

"What was the other thing you said though,
Mr Reynolds. How do you stop making sound
completely?"

"Are there any places where there isn't any sound?"
asks Dara.

Space, I think.

"Well, space is the most obvious one," he says, and
I feel a little proud of myself. "Time for a quick
demonstration?"

Before we can answer, he gets up and wanders over to one of his cupboards full of equipment at the back of the room. After a lot of loud clanging, Mr Reynolds returns with a big glass dome with rubber tubing coming out of one end, and, confusingly, an egg timer.

"So, a place with no sound is called a vacuum," he begins.

"Like a hoover?" asks Stevie.

"Not quite. In a vacuum, like in space, there are no, or very very few, particles to bash together and make vibrations. So there's no sound."

"But then how do people talk in space?" Chia asks.

"By radio waves," Mr Reynolds and I say at the same time.

My cheeks warm a little. I don't want to look like a know-it-all, but I've spent enough time reading about space stations and rockets when I can't sleep that all this information just lives in my head now. Where everyone else has guidance on how to act like a human and be normal, I have endless facts about the moons of Jupiter.

"Vivi, this is going to be loud for a minute," Mr. Reynolds says as he winds up the egg timer. He puts it under the glass dome and attaches the rubber wire to a little tap sticking out of the wall. The egg timer rings inside the dome, and Mr. Reynolds turns the tap at the wall. The sound begins to fade, and fade, until it disappears completely, even though the egg timer is clearly still ringing. We just can't hear it.

"Woahhhh," says Dara. "Did you just suck all the air out?"

"Exactly right."

"Is that why you can't breathe in space?" asks Chia.

"Well, there's no oxygen which is what we need, but yes that's part of it."

"So, just for example, if you sucked away someone's air and they needed air to breathe, they would die?" asks Stevie.

Mr. Reynolds looks briefly worried. "Y-yes."

"Don't mind her. She's just a bit villainy," says Dara cheerily.

"It's just good for me to know there are multiple ways to silence you all when I'm sick of you."

"Okay!" shouts Mr Reynolds nervously. "Maybe that's enough of Science Club today. You guys can go home. Please. Please go home."

*

272

I feel a little bad about maybe making Mr Reynolds regret his career decisions, but I'm grateful we're allowed to leave early. Stevie ushers us all onto a green and white tram, which I'm quietly excited to be riding on. An old lady peers at Gelert with a mix of fear and confusion.

"We need to get a collar for you," I whisper. "A lead too."

"Absolutely not!" he growls.

"You have to wear one, it's the law. People will think I'm a bad owner, or you're a stray. I suppose the second part isn't wrong, but still."

His big hairy brows meet in a frown.

"Someone might try to 'rescue' you, is all."

"I will think about it," he says, with a deep sigh.

I glance back to the woman, hoping she's not reporting him, but luckily she is too engrossed in the very worn book in her hands to pay us any more attention.

We arrive at a wide-open park absolutely filled with people. Two football teams, one in black and one in red, face off in the middle, while parents and friends hop around cheering. To the left is a small café, where dog walkers crowd around drinking hot drinks out of paper cups. Joggers race past us in multicoloured blurs.

It doesn't exactly scream secret hideout.

Stevie sets off in a determined stomp off down a path worn into the grass from walkers. I trot to keep up with her naturally leggy pace, but Dara seems to keep up with no trouble.

"Not that I am questioning your judgement," Dara says. "But isn't this a bit, um . . . full of people?"

Stevie gives them a look, and we follow silently.

The park is much bigger than I first thought. At the top of the hill ahead of us is a thick woodland, and more fields join onto the end of this first one.

Stevie leads us towards a thick cluster of sycamore trees that have grown so close together that their branches interweave. Around their roots is an impenetrable bramble thicket. But when we're right under the trees, I see a tiny cut through which Stevie slips through.

There's a deep basin here, completely hidden from view. At the bottom is a threadbare wooden climbing frame, and a slide leaning at a very unsafe angle. An abandoned playground.

"How did you find this place?" Chia asks, as

I awkwardly shuffle down the steep path.

"Found it when I was little, but I've never seen anyone else here. I come here after training when I want some quiet."

Down here, all sounds from the park disappear. It's like we're enclosed in a bubble, away from the world.

Stevie takes a few things out of her shiny red backpack – a notebook, her pencil case, a stack of cones that she lays out in front of her, and a few bottles of water. She draws a few targets and gives them to Dara to lay out on the hill, which they do before going to inspect the slide covered in peeling paint.

"Do I really have to tell you not to touch those?" Stevie says without looking up. "We don't have time for you to get tetanus or break your arm falling off."

Pouting, Dara raps their knuckle against the slide. A metallic ring sounds. "Just needed to check if it was metal. I'll need to be careful."

"Oh great. *You're* the real safety hazard," laughs Stevie.

"What's the notebook for?" asks Chia, peering over her shoulder at it.

"It's so I can track your progress. I've got sections for each of you," she says, trying to be casual but she's definitely very pleased with herself.

"So our powers can change and grow?" asks Chia wide-eyed with excitement.

"Yeah, Dara's practically ready for a heist now they can take out cameras and unlock doors," I say.

"That's so cool!!!" Chia shrieks. "I wonder what I can do . . ."

"That's what we're here to find out," smiles Stevie.

But first, she makes Dara and I run some drills.

She hands me a bottle of water, and I pull all the liquid into a sphere in my hand. Concentrating hard, I change its shape, so it becomes a long thin rope, and then, with a whipping motion I launch it at a target. It misses, landing in a splash a little too far to the left. I need to practice recalling water, so with a big heave I drag the water, along with a big clod of mud, back towards the bottle. Most of the water goes in. The rest slaps up my leg in a big mucky stain.

"Hmm, precision and control are still issues," Stevie says, writing it down.

"Is *that* important?" I sniff, annoyed that she's grading me on targets when we've literally been fighting monsters.

"Obviously."

With a huff, I grab and relaunch the muddy water at a new target, and, to everyone's surprise, it slices the paper in half.

Dara leaps up and grabs the two halves of the cone. "You've sheared right through it."

"Nice work, Vivi," says Stevie admiringly. "Remember that anger." She gives me a wink and I roll my eyes.

"Good job you're really annoying."

Dara's aim is so much better than mine. They've been practicing a lot too.

I know Stevie and Dara had a practice session alone yesterday, and I would normally feel left out, but whenever they talk about it, they both get shifty and awkward. I don't think anything bad happened; it's more like they're embarrassed that we know they like hanging out together. Weirdos.

It's mesmerising to watch. A spark moves along their pinkish skin to their fingertips. In one fluid motion, their other hand sweeps along their body, like they're drawing a bow ready to fire an arrow. They are beautiful, completely in tune with their powers and their body. Their palm sweeps forward and the spark soars through the air, hitting three of the targets right in the middle.

"Nice work. You're improving," says Stevie.

And at this, their face flushes and they accidentally let loose another spark. It lands right on a cone. A tendril of smoke wafts from it . . . Quickly followed by a flame.

I lob the last of the muddy water at it, and the fire snuffs out. The plastic cone sags, melted completely flat.

"You owe me a cone," Stevie says indignantly.

Chia keels over laughing, followed quickly by Dara. It's contagious, and I find myself flat on my back laughing too.

"Stop laughing, I'm a very serious coaching professional," says Stevie, grinning at us.

Once we've recovered, I ask Dara, "How did you work out how to move like that?"

"Every time I practiced, it just felt right to push it out of me like that. It's not quite pew pew laser guns, but like a dance? Like I'm channelling the electricity through me."

Taking a new bottle from Stevie, I try to copy Dara's movements, but I spin too much, landing in a tangle of limbs. Of course this wouldn't go well:

working out what my body is doing is always hard. Half the time I don't even know if I'm hungry or thirsty, never mind where my limbs are.

Instead of laughing, Stevie helps me to my feet. "Try again, but don't be so Dara about it – think about what works for *your* body. Think about momentum." She stands behind me, takes my wrist in her hand, and she moves my body for me. "This is just going to make sure you don't strain the muscles of your arm." The way the throw moves through my body reminds me of throwing a frisbee on the beach.

I pull a handful of water to me and flatten it into a disc in my palm. Together with Stevie guiding me, we turn, and the disc lands smack in the sizzled-out hole of a target Dara hit.

"Yes!!" shrieks Chia. "Killing it!"

"And now, it's your turn."

A shadow passes over Chia's face. She looks down for a second, takes a breath, and then looks Stevie in the eye, smiling. "I'm ready."

Chapter Twenty-Five

As Dara and I settle down to watch Chia's first session, Gelert joins us from wherever he was roaming. He settles down between us, and I rub the soft velvety tip of his ear with my fingers.

Stevie lowers her voice. "We can go slowly. I just want to see what you can do so far."

"It's okay, I'm ready." Chia almost glows with confidence. It reminds me of what she's like on stage – commanding attention because she knows that she's about to give us a show. "Plus, I accidentally slammed the door shut this morning," she adds with a giggle.

"Think about how you felt when you rescued us," Stevie begins, but stops when she realises that Chia, eyes closed and humming, doesn't need much prompting.

In the centre of her palm forms a perfect miniature tornado, as tall as a pencil. It sways rhythmically, back and forth like algae in the tide. She opens her eyes slowly, and I can tell she knew it would be exactly right from the proud smile she wears.

"Wow," whispers Dara.

"That's a great start," says Stevie, making notes in her playbook. "You've got great control."

"It's like . . . there's a breeze running through me," Chia says.

Stevie watches, pacing around her like a wild creature stalking prey.

"Hold your breath a second, Chia," she asks.

As Chia stops breathing, the tornado stops moving. There's something frozen about it, not the same as the water in my shower, but it's still.

"And start again."

The tornado comes to life again.

"Woah, it's tied to your breath!" cries Dara, clapping their hands. "That's so cool!"

"No wonder you're a natural. Your breath control from singing training is very good," Stevie says.

All that performing in the school and church choirs, plus singing lessons, has given Chia a powerful set of lungs.

"But, as it's tied to the air you're breathing, we will have to be careful to make sure you don't hyperventilate," Stevie adds, scribbling notes in her book.

I am briefly grateful that my powers over water are not connected to the water in my body, or it would get very gross very quickly.

"I was singing when the door slammed," Chia whispers, her palm, snuffing out the tiny tornado. Her eyes are huge and watery. "What if . . . what if singing is broken for me? I don't . . . I don't want that to change too."

Stevie takes her hand. "It won't be. We just need to practice, to separate the two out," she says.

"It does feel different," sniffs Chia.

"Do you need a break?"

"No," she says firmly. "I need to face it."

They go back and forth, making tornados, breathing, and singing a little at a time until she feels the breeze run through her, the edge of her magic. Chia sings in her high, sweet Disney princess voice. Around her feet, the grass stirs, lifting a couple of leaves ever so slightly from the floor. She pauses, steeling herself for just a second, before trying the high notes. Nothing goes flying, and Chia looks so relieved.

Eventually, in her hands appears a swirling cyclone, a flat spiral of white cloudy air. In one quick flowing movement from Chia, the cone is launched high up into the air and out of the den.

All of us are stunned into silence. She's good . . . she's really, really good. And her control is way better than mine is, even now. We are lucky to have her.

"Err, yeah Chia, that'll do it," whispers Stevie.

"I'll retrieve your cone." Gelert gets to his feet abruptly, knocking Dara and I over in the process.

Chia bounces on her heels, a small tornado weaving between her fingers. "It makes sense to me." She spins in a pirouette, and the rest of the cones fall one by one. There's a confidence in her movements, like she's being doing this forever.

And her aim isn't just good. It's perfect.

Gelert appears and drops the cone in his mouth next to me. He looks at where all the cones were only seconds ago, and sighs. "I'll go get those as well I suppose."

Stevie sits down next to us in the grass as Chia dances with joy. "Wow she's making you look bad," she murmurs.

"I am *completely* fine with that," I say, truthfully.

Chia crashes down next to us, a little out of breath.

"You okay?" asks Stevie.

"Yeah, I'm good. It's like the most breath I've ever had. I'm tired out now though." She lies back in the cool grass, breathing slow and deep into her chest.

"I bet now you could belt the loudest note ever heard. Only slightly louder than you were before," teases Stevie.

"I'll be heard across the world!"

"Space too."

"Wait!" cries Dara, grabbing my arm tightly. "That's it. Space. Vacuums! Chia if you are this powerful already, maybe we can try . . . I need to go." They scrabble to their feet. "I have to go invent."

Stevie stills them with a hand. "Tomorrow. First, pizza."

Their eyes light up. "Pizza?"

"Pizza."

*

It turns out that Stevie lives just up the road from the park, in a huge house.

"Are your parents home?" Chia asks, and then adds, "Wait, have you taken these two to your house before? Big step, Stevie."

"No. Papa's working late, and Maman is out with some yoga friends," she sniffs, ignoring any suggestion she might have opened up to us.

"Wait, why didn't we train in your mum's home studio?"

"Wait, you have a gym *at home*?" gasps Dara.

"You've seen their aim," Stevie says to Chia, ignoring Dara's outbursts. "I didn't want to have to explain why all the exercise mats were covered in scorch marks."

We order pizza and it arrives in the blink of an eye. That's one bit of London I could get used to.

All four of us flop down on the big couches in the living room, with a huge slice of melty cheese pizza each.

In between bites, Chia asks us about how our powers have grown and changed, and Dara tells her all about the doors and cameras at the British Library.

"I'm still just excited that I can do *anything* that it's hard to imagine it could grow, like become more than just lobbing bottles of water at monsters,"

I say, pulling a long thread of cheese with my fingers. "I've never been sporty, apart from swimming and winning the odd egg-and-spoon race; I'm not used to my body doing things I actually want it to."

Purple light traces the skin on Dara's palm. "This is the first time I've felt really connected to my body. Sewing cool clothes helps a bit, helps me see myself, you know? Sometimes I get so clouded by what other people think they see when they look at me that I can't tell which thoughts are mine and which are theirs. But with this?" The light glows softly. "There's no doubt. It's just part of me."

I don't think I'd ever met a non-binary person before Dara, but my Mums had obviously taught me a lot about LGBTQ+ people and had impressed on me that we all had to look out for each other. We'd been lucky that no one had made life too hard for us, though they forever asked if my Mums were sisters. Some people have it a lot, lot harder than just whispers and the occasional rude comment.

"I get that," says Stevie. 'You wouldn't believe how many people have asked me 'what are you?' or 'how Asian are you?'. It's not for them to say. I'm mixed. It doesn't matter how much of either."

"That must be really difficult to deal with," says Dara.

"I get that too. Where are you from? *No, where are you really from?*" sighs Chia. "Like, I don't know you. Stop asking for my biography, you weirdos."

"It sucks, doesn't it," agrees Stevie. "For me, it's either that, or people take one look at my little arm and just see what *they* think is missing, what they think I can't do. Or they'll ask how I can even blow my nose, or button a shirt. But there's nothing missing, this is how my body has always been. I use prosthetics for some sports because they help, but everything else I can do just as well as everyone else can, just in my own way."

They look at me, and I know that they're waiting for me to share. To tell them what it's really like to be autistic, at least for me. I know they'll have picked up some bits from just being around me, but there's so much more that people who aren't autistic don't see. I'm scared, but I have to trust them with this part of me – like I trust them with my life.

"A lot of people assume that because I'm autistic, I don't have my own thoughts or really know what I want, partly because sometimes it takes me a little longer to process stuff. Some of them think I don't feel anything at all and that my opinion doesn't matter because of that."

Stevie growls, and I am pretty sure it's about how people have treated me, rather than the pizza.

"Other people think I'm totally incapable. Or they expect me to have some genius superpower talent . . . which, well, in this case I guess I do, but that's not because I'm autistic. It's all extremes and when you add it all up, it's like they don't see me as a person." I pull gently at my plait, and run the end through my fingers, which settles the buzzing energy in my body. "I'm not broken. I'm just wired differently."

We are all quiet for a moment, taking in each other's stories.

"Hell is other people," says Dara and we all laugh with relief. "Everyone but us. We have each other, right?"

It's lovely, but also terrifying. I have friends, I realise. Actual good friends. And even though I'm scared, even though there's that buzz underneath it all that means I'm slightly on edge all the time, I'm starting to trust that they really do care about me.

"Hands in?" says Dara. I hold out my hand, and they place theirs on top of mine. Stevie and Chia add theirs on top. Before we can throw up our hands and shout something inspirational, a spark shoots through our skin. We all leap back giggling and yelping all at once.

"Sorry!!" cries Dara. "It always happens when I'm nervous, or like, emotional. You get it." They rub their hand on their chest to get rid of the static.

"We should decide what to shout this time," I say.

"To friends?" Dara offers.

"To friends," I whisper back.

"To friends *and* adventures," says Chia.

"Yes, yes, to friends," says Stevie. "Enough mushy stuff, I don't want you going soft on me. You're supposed to be warriors."

"Warriors can be soft too," protests Dara.

"In touch with our emotions and able to kick butt," Chia adds.

We watch some silly videos on YouTube until all the pizza is gone, and then make plans. Tomorrow is going to be another busy day. Dara and Chia agree to work on the vacuum ideas together after school, while Stevie insists I need a fencing lesson. I reluctantly agree, knowing that she's right. At the moment my powers are only useful if there's water, and it would be silly to have an enchanted sword and not know how to use it properly, even if I did do a decent job of stabbing one coraniaid.

It feels like we're getting closer to where we need to be. The four of us together, united, and ready to venture into the Unlands on a rescue mission. Find the kids first, and the next calon, somehow.

For once, I don't feel completely terrified. Not with them at my side.

Chapter Twenty-Six

Thursday night is always games night at home, so I leave once we've made our plans. It's an easy ride back on the tram to my house, and I feel a swell in my chest as I realise, I actually feel at home here. I'm a person who just casually gets a tram now.

At home, Mumma sits at the kitchen table surrounded by paint charts, while Mam makes a round of tea.

"Hey peanut. Did you have a good time at the park?" Mam asks, kissing me on the forehead.

"Yes thanks."

"What do you think about these colours for the living room?" Mumma asks, holding up two pots of paint that, even to me, look like the same shade of green.

I try to just look enthusiastic and smile which is what she and Mam do when I talk about my latest special interest. "They look nice Mumma," I say, giving her a thumbs up.

"Ready to be beaten to a pulp today?" asks Mam with a wink, and, while I know she means the board games, it feels a little on the nose.

"Heh, yeah," I say, before taking a big gulp of air. "Can I talk to you both about something, please?"

They both switch into concerned parent mode. Paint charts are swept aside for steaming cups, as Mam and I both sit down.

"This is going to sound weird, or maybe you won't believe me because of what has happened before," I begin slowly. "But I want you to listen to me and trust what I'm saying."

"Okay bach, we will" says Mumma, and they both nod like plastic dogs on a car dashboard.

"What I want to say is that . . . I'm okay. I have good friends who look out for me, and it's different from last time because I know what a good friend looks like now."

Mam adjusts her glasses, her eyes glossy.

"There are always going to be meltdowns. You

taught me that life is about things changing and learning to adapt and growing. Sometimes I'm going to find that hard, but it doesn't mean I shouldn't *do it*."

Mumma presses her lips together in a firm line, and twines her fingers through Mam's, their rings clacking together.

"I'm safe. And you can trust me to tell you when things aren't okay."

The last line stings sour as I say it. Because yes, maybe I would tell them if I was ever bullied again, and that's really what I'm talking about now.

But also, things are not really *okay*, in like normal people terms. Most people aren't training to maybe save a load of missing children, hunt down reborn witches and prevent imminent disaster, but still.

I can't tell them about that part. They'd try to protect me. This is me protecting them.

"We trust you," croaks Mumma. They're both crying but it's happy tears. "We're so proud of you."

"After the last few years at school . . . we didn't think it was going to be easy for you, coming down here. All the moving and the change. But you've done so well." says Mam.

"You've been so strong," adds Mumma. "And we are so happy you've found a really lovely group of friends who care about you."

"And who you were brave enough to open your heart to. That can't have been easy for you."

"We are very proud of you, Vivi."

"Thanks," I say. My cheeks flush with heat, a little embarrassment mixed with semi-related lying agony.

We curl up in a big cuddle together.

"I'm sorry if we were a bit overprotective," says Mumma, wiping away a snotty tear. "We just . . ."

"Don't want me to be back there again, I know. But things are different."

I smell the tiniest hint of sulphur, and through the glass of the backdoor, I can see Gelert watching us as my Mums clutch me. What if he came to live with us? What if I told the Mums about him, made them think he was just a normal dog we found, and that he could live here? I don't know how taking him to the vet would work, but maybe no one would realise he's a ghost dog if he was around all the time. It would mean he'd have a place to live.

He's dedicated his life to us; it seems like the least I could do.

After school, I go home with Stevie for my first lesson with Excalibur.

There really is an exercise studio in her basement. One wall is lined in mirrors, and the other houses a weight stand, with a neat stack of yoga mats in the corner.

"Is it okay that I'm down here? I don't want to break anything."

"I can handle just one of you. You and Dara together is too much chaos at once."

She disappears to a cupboard at the back of the room. From my rucksack, I draw out Excalibur, wrapped in a thick woollen scarf. I should probably find a better way of transporting it, but asking my Mums to buy me a scabbard might give the game away.

Stevie returns holding two long thin fencing swords, dressed from head to toe in white kit.

"Er, no, you can put that away for now. I don't fancy practicing with you wielding an actual weapon."

She places the swords on the floor, and from the cupboard returns with some spare bits of kit; a mesh fronted helmet which she informs me is called a mask, a plastic chest plate, and a jacket that's a little too long in the arms. I suspect the latter bits belong to her mum as I'm quite a lot chubbier than Stevie and wouldn't fit in anything she owned. It's okay once I've rolled the sleeves up. It has a weird strap that goes in-between your legs, which she has to do up for me after I almost fall over trying to do it myself.

"Is there any sport you don't do?" I ask genuinely.

"Probably not. I'm good at them all," she sighs, as though it's a burden to be so talented.

She stands me in front of the mirror, without a sword to start with.

"Lesson one: stance," she says. It turns out that there are important ways to stand for fencing, and presumably for all sword fighting. She adjusts my body, so my back is straight as a line, knees bent slightly, and feet at ninety degrees.

"Do I really need to stand like this for Excalibur? In the books it was always a two-handed sword," I say.

"True but, here me out. First, it's much smaller than in the books. It's not too heavy, right?" I nod. "Second, you use your hands with your magic, so you need at least one free."

"That's actually very smart," says Gelert, who appears sitting on top of inflatable exercise ball. "Who'd have thought?"

"I don't like how surprised you sound."

The dog says nothing else, just admires himself in the mirror, so Stevie gives the ball he lies on a little kick. "Oi, steady on," he says, legs akimbo.

"We might have to think about training you to use one left-handed," she murmurs, looking at my stance. "Probably the water if you're right-handed. We'll practice that after."

"I can try," I say, and then thinking of Chia's confidence I add, "I can do that."

Stevie gives me a satisfied grin.

We run drills. It turns out that aiming your sword is really hard. Never mind parrying someone else's attack. And that's before you even learn to hit back, a *riposte*. The more we do it, I can feel something click into place in my head. My muscles are tired, but the more we practice, the more I realise I'm actually good at this.

We take a break and I drink down a huge bottle of water.

"How's she doing, eh?" I hear Gelert ask Stevie.

"Good. Far better than I expected for someone who hasn't fenced and she's learning quickly. I was expecting her to be much worse for longer," she says, and I know there's a compliment in there somewhere. "No offence."

"None taken," I say. "It does feel natural. Like, I know this isn't a sport but all other sporty things I've been rubbish at."

"Could be the connection," suggests Gelert. "You, Nimuë, the sword. Perhaps the bond makes it easier?"

"Or she's a cold-blooded killer underneath it all."

"Ha! Chance would be a fine thing."

The two of them laugh about this for longer than I think is necessary.

"What brings you to the gym, Gel?" I ask, but before I can continue, the doorbell goes and he vanishes.

When Stevie returns with Dara and Chia he reluctantly reappears.

"I bring some bad news. The portal has closed," he says.

"You're sure?" I ask.

"Sure as there's not a blinking great hole there anymore."

"Damn," mutters Stevie.

"There has to be another nearby," says Chia. "It's such a warren in there, but there must be other portals for the coraniaids to get in and out easily. The one that took me didn't take me straight to the Unlands – it dragged me through a portal first."

"Possibly, but we'd have to find it."

Slowly, an idea forms in my head. "Do you think the portals are closed for good?"

Gelert is quiet for a little while as he thinks. "No. It's like a door, right?"

He gets up and nudges the door to the studio closed. "When it's closed to your world, it disappears."

"But in the Unlands, you'd still see the doorway," finishes Chia.

"Right that is."

"So we just need to find a way to open it."

That confirms it then, I think. I don't want to say it out loud, because it's *horrible*, and could definitely go wrong, but the plan in my head is the only one I can think of.

And to my surprise, Stevie says exactly what I was thinking. "Plan B. We bait them into taking me."

"No, we absolutely cannot do that," says Dara firmly.

"Yes, we can. Listen, they keep appearing where

we are. I don't know which of us they're after, but hopefully they'll come if I wait for them. We can go back to where we know the portal is. And, if they take me, hopefully the portal will open up long enough for you to follow."

"No way." Dara shakes their head. "We are not putting you in danger. You're important to this team."

"Well obviously," she says, rolling her eyes. "But let's be smart about this, Dara. If we use one of you as bait, then we're down a power. I've been to the Unlands before, I know what I'm in for."

Dara shakes their head.

"It has to be me."

I hate that she's right, and how calm she is about it.

"Okay," I agree.

"Are you two both losing it?" cries Dara. "This is ridiculous."

"It's my choice," says Stevie. "Gelert agrees, don't you?"

"The girl is the best choice. But, so you don't all get your knickers in a twist, I'll follow her in. Maybe I can stay out of sight and help you all reunite inside."

"Are you up to that?" I ask, not wanting to outright

300

call him old and feeble but he basically slept for days after taking me to Wales.

"Don't coddle me, froglet," he snarls. "We all have a part to play."

"Urgh! I hate this!!" shouts Dara.

"We know. I think everyone in London knows by now too." Stevie sidles over and shoulder bumps Dara, dropping her voice low to say, "Don't be upset with me."

"I'm not. I just . . . I don't want you in danger."

I turn away from what feels like an intensely private moment between them.

"Can we show you what we came up with instead?" asks Chia, and I'm so grateful for her changing the topic.

Reluctantly, Dara gets out what I expect is going to be their new invention. Instead, it's a Bluetooth speaker.

"Remember how Mr. Reynolds showed us how a vacuum can make the sound disappear? We realised that if Chia can make one, we can limit the sound we make when we're walking around the Unlands. The coraniaids won't even know we're there."

"How?" Stevie asks.

"Vacuums are places with no air particles. Moving them around is basically how her magic works. So if she can move the air—"

"Then she can move the sound," I finish.

"But if there's no air, how will we breathe?" asks Stevie.

"I've been trying to concentrate it. Like a bubble," Chia says.

"Demo time?" asks Dara excitedly.

"Demo time." She plugs her phone into the speakers, which plays her repeating the words "hey monsters, come and get me" over and over. The sound is tinny, scratchy in my head.

"Do me a favour and all take a big breath first before I do this . . . just in case," she adds which is pretty ominous.

Holding my breath is easy for me thanks to swimming. Beside me, Dara fidgets and starts to go pink. I'm about to suggest we stop, but then I realise the ache has gone from my head. The air around the speaker shines ever so slightly. There's no sound.

And Chia looks very, very pleased with herself.

We all let go of our breaths in a rush of *wows*. The speaker sits in a bubble of vacuum, swallowing the sound up.

"Is there a way you could make one around us?" I ask, poking at the bubble. It doesn't pop, holding firm.

"It can't be around us completely, or we'll asphyxiate," points out Dara.

"I was thinking for the tunnels, maybe some kind of barrier? Or shield? Something to stop our sound going ahead to them. I don't think I could hold two at once so the risk is something coming behind us would hear."

Dara nods. "It's not perfect, but it could work."

"Let's practice," agrees Chia.

"We just need to agree one more thing," says Stevie, capturing our attention. "Let's go tomorrow evening. My parents are away all weekend. Everyone tell your parents you're staying here to work on Dara's play. And in the evening when it's quiet, we go. That gives us enough time in case things take longer than we expect."

"That's not a lot of time to prepare," I say with a sigh.

"I don't think we have much choice," counters Chia. "Time moves so much faster there. And I don't think anyone else got out, did they?"

I shake my head. I'd been checking *Strange Britain* all week just in case someone found a news article or a Facebook post or anything, and there's been nothing. It's always possible that their parents don't remember they were even missing, like with Chia's, but surely *someone* would remember. We remembered she was gone, after all.

"Unless the coraniaids have been bringing food and water for them . . ." She trails off, and that seals it really. If this is the first opportunity we have to save them, we have to take it.

"Tomorrow it is," says Dara.

Chapter Twenty-Seven

I wake to find myself by Nimuë's pool. She sits at my feet, making a daisy chain out of small white flowers.

"Hello," I say, joining her on the grass.

"Hello." It feels like a lifetime ago that I was last here, but it's only been a few days. The cold fresh air reminds me of Wales. In London, it just tastes different. Less salt, less sheep poo. More pollution but also much more fried chicken. Ups and downs.

"It feels so long since I last saw you. So much has happened. How does this work anyway? Like do you summon me or . . ?"

"It is a two-way connection. I do not drag you here," she says. "But I could sense you were very tired. I hoped you would come when you were ready, but

I was worried you wouldn't come back."

"Why?"

"Because I probably would not return had someone just told me to get on with it."

I dig my toes into the soft grass. "To be honest, I think I needed the pep talk."

"Oh. Good."

She doesn't ask me how I am, or really try to continue the conversation. Just keeps linking daisies. Eventually she hands me a small pile of flowers, and I pick up a few to make my own. My nails are bitten short, not ideal for lacing flowers. The stems smush together, and I drop them in my lap.

I realise she is probably waiting for me to update her on what's happening to me, in the real world. Outside of this . . . dream, or whatever it is.

I tell her first about Stevie. When I tell her that Stevie is, in summary, a little scary, thinks she's always right, but is very effective at training, she snorts. It's this glassy twinkling noise, rather than my impression of a full-grown wild boar. "Oh yes. Yes, I'm deeply familiar with that type of person."

Even water fairies have to deal with know-it-all's, it seems.

"But we did find the next calon," I say, and her eyes light up. "I mean, she did get kidnapped by coraniaids and was hidden in the Unlands, but we got her back."

"Who?" she asks, blinking at this rush of information. "Rhiannon?"

She takes this in with a nod. "You know, she was the first person I went to about all this."

This surprises me. I always presumed Ceridwen was the one who organised it all, like Dara had to. But apparently it was Nimuë, and in turn me. If Gelert had come to me first, I'm not sure I would've gone along with it all.

"What's she like?"

"She is brave, and always surprising. A little reserved sometimes, but that is perhaps how life changes you. There's a quiet wildness to her. A path of her own to follow." She turns to me, "Do you know how Arawn became so enamoured with the human world?"

I shake my head.

"Many years ago, a human named Pwyll stumbled into Annwn. His dogs followed a stag, and unbeknownst to them, travelled through a portal to

Annwn."

I shiver, thinking of the way the portal felt against my skin. "I don't know how he missed that."

"I can't imagine either," she says with a laugh. "Of course, he only realised he was in Annwn once he had killed the stag on Arawn's land. And killing a creature on another man's land is—"

"Uh oh."

"Uh oh indeed, but Arawn was amused as much as he was annoyed and so he proposed a deal."

"Isn't 'don't make a deal with Otherworld creatures' like the first rule?"

"Yes, but the reason you know that is because of stories like this."

"Good point. What was the deal?"

"That they would swap lives for a year, and that Pwyll would go to battle Arawn's enemy Hafgan, a King of another part of the Other. He agreed, and they swapped lives. Disguised as Pwyll, Arawn lived in the human world. When their deal was over, Pwyll went back to the human world, and they parted as friends and allied Kings."

"That's a wild story."

"It is."

"Did no one notice?"

"Not a single person."

"So how does Rhiannon come into this?"

"Pwyll saw her riding in the human world one day, and instantly fell in love with her. She really is very beautiful. His riders could never catch up to her, and one day when he went to visit Arawn, he saw her riding through Annwn, and so he approached her."

"If she was in Annwn, does that mean she's like you? Not human, I mean."

"Yes, she is Tylwyth Teg. Or fey if you prefer."

"So did they get married?"

"Eventually. She was betrothed to another, but that's another story. The thing you need to know is that her life was not always easy – people accused her of killing her own child and for seven years she apologised for a crime she did not commit. And eventually, Pwyll died. Once his loyalty to Pwyll was gone, Arawn decided he'd rather take your world for his own. And that is how it all began."

"That must have been hard for her, going against her dead husband's friend."

"Challenging your family, whether it be blood or chosen, is no easy task."

I let this sink in for a moment.

"Chia is probably the nicest person I've ever met."

"Well, that sounds like a good addition to your team." Her eyes get misty, or mistier I suppose, lost in memory. "Three of six of us already. You, and Ceridwen and Rhiannon . . ."

"Dara and Chia," I correct. "And Stevie. I really thought she was going to be a calon too. It must be hard for her."

"She will find her own place, in time. Do not worry about that. It is hard to be wrong about something when you are used to being right."

We sit quietly again. Nimuë's running out of white flowers to link in a chain, so I start picking ones around me to add to her pile.

I feel like now I should tell her the harder bits.

"We're going back to the Unlands tomorrow."

Her translucent skin pales. "What do you mean *going back*?"

"I've been there before," I say.

The flowers in her lap spills as she reaches for me, her hands hovering just above my skin, as though she wants to touch me but can't decide if she *can*.

"We've been a few times, actually. That's how we

310

got Chia back. Or rather, she saved us. And we found a way to navigate round using the crystals, thanks to this guy called Emrys."

Her eyes widen, just a fraction. "Did you say Emrys?" she whispers.

"Yes? His name is familiar, but I don't really know why. I think there's a mountain named that?"

"Named after him," she mutters, but moves ahead before I can question this. "That man . . . or boy as I imagine he presented to you?"

I confirm this with a nod.

"He is the wizard Myrddin. Or you might know him as Merlin. And you must be very, very careful with what he says."

"Merlin?" I gasp. I didn't think I had the any shock left in me, but there it is. Apparently, Merlin *the wizard* has been talking to me. At the same time, I feel kind of silly for being surprised. Of course he's real. I have the sword and I'm standing talking to Nimuë. He's a part of those stories, and I guess this world, as much as the other names I've ended up recognising.

It's just . . . He's *Merlin*. He's a Disney character.

"Be careful with him," Nimuë warns, snapping me

out of my confusion. "I fear this will not be the only time you meet him, unfortunately. I was hoping he'd keep clear, have something better to do for once."

"Is he . . . not a friend of yours?" I ask, trying to remember the stories they're in together but coming up blank.

"What is a friend or foe when you speak of a man who only moves to his own desires?" she snarls.

I don't quite understand what she means, but I take this as a warning to not trust the guy. "I'll be careful."

"Good."

We set about picking up all the flower heads which are strewn around us. I think about how Chia could gather them with just a breath, and then realise I haven't shown Nimuë my powers. I didn't even think about whether I could use them here.

Without a word, I pull a rope of water from the pool towards me, curling it around and over us like a fountain.

Her face breaks open into a huge smile, and I feel her pull the water from my hands into her grasp. With a flick, the water turns into intricate snowflakes which hang in the air, then slowly glide down to us.

I catch one on my tongue.

There's so much more for me to learn. Maybe one day I will be this powerful.

I yawn, and the familiar slipping fade rises in me. I'm leaving, perhaps going back to sleep proper or waking up.

"Goodbye Vivi, for now." She says it softly, a little sad.

"Keep calling me. I like coming here," I tell Nimuë.

Nimuë visibly brightens, sparkles running through her hair. "Have a good day Vivi. Say hello to the other calonnau for me."

Chapter Twenty-Eight

I've never been a very good liar, but the Mums barely question the sudden sleepover we decide to have. Thankfully, they don't ask me about how the play is going. They seem to have just accepted that this might be my new thing. To my relief, they didn't ask to call Stevie's parents either, else we'd have to have Gelert pretend to be her dad.

Seeing as Chia's mum is still spelled so doesn't even realise she was missing, there's no issue with her coming. Dara's Mum is away at a conference for her architecture studies and their Pops is working late, meaning their older brother Rabbie is supposed to keep an eye on Dara. Luckily, they found out that Rabbie is planning on sneaking out to a party of his own so Dara cut a deal: they won't tell the parents that Rabbie's out if Rabbie doesn't say anything about Dara going to Stevie's. And Lachie gets a takeaway and a quiet night at home alone.

I decide not to ask the Mums about Gelert until I'm back home. After all, I don't really know for certain that I'm coming back, as much as I don't want to think about that.

"I just finished tumble-drying your best jarms." Mam places the neatly folded flannel pjs on my bed, next to my open sleepover bag. Luckily, I haven't yet put in the things I need for our actual adventure: a big bottle of water, Excalibur, warm dark clothing so we can sneak into the park.

"Thanks Mam."

She places a kiss on the top of my head, before heading back downstairs. I can hear them talking, speaking in soft, proud voices I normally only hear when I've done something really good. It's nice.

I flip open my tablet and start a new message to the Ghost Queen who seems to be online. She might not officially be part of the team, but I feel like after all the help she gave us with the British Library I owe her an update.

Hello. Are you there?

The adventurer returns. How goes it?

Umm, well.
We just wanted to give you an update.
We managed to get into the archives and found the
pamphlet you told us about.

I pause, realising I should probably have thought
about the fact that these messages detail at least a
handful of crimes.

Excellent work.
Did it contain the knowledge you sought?

Yes, you were right. The monsters are coraniaids.
And they have been taking the stolen children.

Do you have any insight into why?

I want to tell her. I do. But if I do, then I have to
tell her about Arawn and the spell and Gelert and that
I'm not just using Nimuë as a secret identity. Maybe

when all this is over, when we've found all the calonnau and defeated Arawn, I can explain everything. But until then, I'm going to have to hope she still wants to work with me.

I really want to explain everything, but I can't just yet.

But we're going to stop the coraniaids and rescue the others.

I hope.

The Ghost Queen doesn't answer for a few minutes, clearly thinking this through, and honestly, I don't really blame her. All she's got from this relationship is the knowledge that some magical stuff is really happening, but she is the one who has been helping us find out what's happening. She's the brains of the operation.

How do you know they have the children still?

I don't, for certain.
But we know roughly where they were and hopefully they are all still there. I wanted to tell you what was happening so that you knew. So that someone knew. In case we can't get back.

I probably shouldn't say this much but I'm so scared and I feel the need to tell her, because I can't tell my parents, and Dara, Stevie and Chia certainly keep skirting past it. There's no one else I can say this to. And they and the rest of the people on the forum will just have to be our backup.

Nimuë I sense this is part of a much greater plan than just yourself. You speak much of 'we' in a way that I think is more than just yourself and "Ceridwen" And so I will trust that one day we can share the truth of the matter. Until then, I will continue to help you, where I can. We can be helpful to each other, while also strangers. Of a kind.

I swear the weirdest bit of all this magic stuff isn't the magic or monsters; it's just how everyone speaks to me. Vagueness and dancing around the truth. I get the sense that that 'of a kind' means that Ghost Queen knows more about me than I do about her. Hopefully that's not a bad thing. Either way, it's something I'll have to deal with later.

Thanks. I mean it.

We need every ally we can get.

Good luck, Nimuë.

I have a feeling we will speak again.

The Ghost Queen goes offline, and I sit for a moment thinking about what's ahead of me. Not just tonight, this is still the beginning of the journey. Sure, we could bring all the stolen children home, but we've got more people to find, more battles to fight.

I should be tired, but somehow, I'm not.

I'm as ready as I'll ever be.

I hold Excalibur for a moment, letting the steel shine in the light.

"I'm going Nimuë. Wish us luck," I whisper.

The sword hums against my skin like a promise.

*

Mam drops me off at Stevie's where, as soon as she lets me in the door, she disappears off into another room, muttering under her breath.

I wander towards the lounge and find Chia camped out on the couch. She pats the space next to her.

'And now, we wait,' she says, as I sit down.

'What's up with Stevie?'

'She's checking we've got everything we need. I mean, we're not really taking much so I don't know what she's packing. When she last came through she was chanting granola bar granola bar granola bar.'

'Do you think she'll be okay?'

Chia nods. 'We had a good chat about the Unlands, before you got here. I wanted her to know everything I knew if she's going to be there without us, though hopefully not for long.'

I think of Chia alone in the Unlands for days and days.

'Are you okay about going back in?'

'I am, and I'm not, if that makes sense? It's such a fascinating place. There really is nowhere else like it, and I got to see that and explore it. And Eirlys, she's there too, though I'm not going to call for her today. She's hardly kitted out for battle,' she says with a smile.

'We can put that on Dara's list of things to make: magical horse armour.'

Something passes across her face, and the smile fades. 'But then, I was also alone, for days. Or stuck with a bunch of other frightened kids. That part wasn't magical, and I do not want to be trapped again.'

'We won't lose you,' I tell her, and she reaches out for my hand. I let her take it.

'I know. I don't think Stevie would let you leave without me anyway.'

'What was that?' she says, stomping past with bottles full of water.

'Just talking about how much you loooooove me,' Chia teases.

'I think we should leave her there this time,' Stevie shouts from the other room, but we all know she's joking. No one gets left behind.

'I'll be okay, I'm ready,' she says, squeezing my hand. 'I might just need a moment when we're in there.'

'Whatever you need,' I say.

Without another word, Chia flicks on the TV and we sink back into the couch to watch cartoons. After a couple of episodes, Dara arrives.

We eat fried rice splashed with extra bright red crispy chilli oil, out of takeaway containers at the kitchen table. None of us want to eat really, our stomachs too jumbled with nerves, but depending on what happens tonight, this could be our last meal for a while. We share around prawn toast and lumpia, and I once again am glad to live somewhere where all this food comes at the press of a button (and a parents' credit card).

Typically, Gelert appears as we're eating, and Dara makes up a bowl of the best bits for him. He digs into it happily, his great big tail wagging slowly. Note to self: feed the ghost dog.

Once the table is clear and our bellies full, we go over the plan.

On their phone, Dara opens a map of the park, showing a huge track of forest, wide expansive fields and then at the top of one of them, a big white building like an old house. I don't remember much from being there the first time, so I'm glad we have this to look at.

The plan is this: Stevie will go ahead alone, trailed through the aether by Gelert. Chia, Dara and I will hide up on the balcony of a big white house building that looks over the whole park. Chia will cover the noise, while Dara and I are on fighting duty. When they take Stevie, we follow her in. Hopefully.

All we need is the coraniaids to take the bait.

To take Stevie.

While we'd been watching cartoons, Stevie made up care packages for us all. Bottles of water and snacks for everyone, matches, paper and pencil to leave notes, plasters and bandage tape. She really had thought of everything. The kits are packed up into zip-up bags and she hands one to each of us to add to our backpacks.

We change out of our normal clothes into thick layers of black clothes, which will definitely look weird on the tram but hopefully will keep us warm enough.

The last trams leave around 10.30, so we decide to leave then, hoping it looks like we're headed home from something, rather than sneaking out.

'I've made something for Gelert,' Dara says, holding out a temporary collar made from an old leather belt. Gelert seems much more willing to try this than the red and white polka dot lead of Cally's that they also brought, but makes no more complaints; he knows, just like we do, that we need everything to go right, and being stopped by a dog warden is going to muck everything up.

It turns out Dara didn't just make accessories for Gelert. There must be no leather left in their house at this point – all of it repurposed for our mission. They hold out another belt, this time for me.

'I was thinking of having them hang from your shoulders, a kind of cross body thing, but I was too worried you'd get tangled, or it gave monsters too much opportunity to just grab you,' they say as they fit it round me.

Slung in against my left hip is a scabbard for Excalibur, the perfect place for using it right-handed.

And nestled sturdily on my other hip is a bottle, that pops open with a buttoned lid, for easily accessible water.

'Dara, this is amazing,' I say.

'See, an awl can be useful,' they say pointedly at Stevie, who just rolls her eyes.

With my weapons on me, I feel like a real warrior. Even if I'll have to be really careful not to explode the water if I panic.

"And I brought this," they say, brandishing a new and improved version of the net gun we tested in their back garden. The net is folded neatly, but I can tell it's huge now, and the whole thing looks heavy.

"Are you okay to carry that?" asks Chia.

They flex their arms. "Obviously."

It would have been sensible to get a nap in before we left, but all of us are wired. We watch more cartoons, snacking on gummy sweets. We all try not to pay attention to the clock.

When it's finally time, we do final toilet trips and checks of our bags before heading out, via a blissfully empty tram.

We get off earlier than the main entrance, where we know the gates will be locked anyway. Following the map and Stevie, we head down a tiny walker's path that goes through a very muddy bit of forest and eventually will open into the park itself. I let Gelert off the lead and he shakes his fur, relieved.

At the edge of the forest, we all stop in a line. In front of us, the park opens up into a wide expanse of grass.

Chia shivers next to me.

"Are you cold?" I ask, keeping my voice low. 'Do you need another jumper?'

She shakes her head. "No, I'm fine. Just a bit scared."

I offer her my hand, and she takes it. Her skin is warm against my permanently cold hands.

"Are you ready?" Chia asks Stevie, who stares ahead at the open park.

"Yeah, I am. Consider this your ultimate training session team. Rescue the coach." She laughs softly.

"There's still time for us to change the plan," whispers Dara, their voice wobbling.

"No, this is how it's got to be," says Stevie, turning to face them. Something passes between them, and Dara eventually nods, sighing.

Gelert raises his head to the air and sniffs. His great tail wags.

They're here.

I reach for Gelert and scratch his ears, as if to say *don't do anything heroic and keep Stevie safe*. He licks my palm very softly just once, then realises what he's doing. Embarrassed, he disappears on the spot.

"Ready?" Stevie mouths.

Chia smiles, I give a thumbs up. Dara puffs out their cheeks and gives another tiny nod.

A tiny smirk plays across Stevie's lips. "Come and get me," she whispers.

And with that, she runs into the night.

Her footsteps crunch in the leaves, but we lose the sound of her as soon as she disappears into the black up ahead.

Just the three of us remain. We take our time following the route towards the big house, careful not to stray off the path into the clumps of nettles that line it. The big white building looms up ahead, eerily lit in green security lighting.

We crawl up the steps on our hands and knees, Dara leading the way. The balcony is so cold, in the path of a particularly chilly breeze. I almost want to ask Chia to use her power to stop it.

In the field below us stands a dark figure. Stevie.

We wait. And wait.

Just as I'm starting to worry that this is not going to work, I catch a very familiar sound carried on the wind. A coraniaid is here.

Dara points to one of the huge oak trees in the far distance. The air changes, suddenly shining, shimmering. It's the portal, though it's in a different position from last time. Maybe it's a new entrance to the nest. I hope it is.

It all happens in seconds.

The coraniaid jumps. Stevie screams. And the two of them disappear right through the portal in a whisp of smoke.

Chapter Twenty-Nine

We run faster that I've ever run before. Chia's nails dig into my palm. We have to reach the portal before it closes.

The shining portal still hangs in the air as we reach it, and, one after another, we dive in headfirst.

We land in a heap. Quick as a flash, Chia throws a vacuum barrier down the tunnel to mask the sound of us untangling. It's a strange breathless moment, like she's sucked the air out of my chest.

The caves are strangely familiar to me now, though I don't actually recognise where we've landed. It is a new tunnel. The eerie blue glow of the crystals lights our faces enough for us to see. This part of the cave system is darker, I'm almost certain of it.

With a palm of sparks, Dara leads the way, followed

by Chia who moves the vacuum barrier along as we walk to mask our footsteps. I'm last. My hand grips so hard on Excalibur's hilt that my fingers ache.

We pick our way quietly through the damp darkness. I search the walls for our markers, but there are none. I don't know where we are.

After a few minutes, we reach a crossroads. Dara looks back, unsure where to go either.

While I might not have been this way before, Chia might have. I tap Chia's shoulder and sign "Which?", and she steps around carefully, inspecting all our options. I wonder how long she was wandering the Unlands trying to get out.

Chia reluctantly points to one path where the tunnel slopes downwards, like a route into the belly of some horrible beast.

The slope gets steeper and narrower as we walk. And soon it's so steep that we have to pick our way down sideways, like I had to do when Mam would take us hiking up in the mountains. It takes us ages to get anywhere, and in the back of my mind all I can hear is Stevie begging us to hurry up.

At least, I'm pretty sure it's in my mind.

Before I can think anymore, I lose my footing, and

skid on my feet. Chia spins and grabs hold of me, and together we crash into Dara's back. Their hands fling out against the tunnel walls, and luckily we all stop before we can slide down the tunnel. It's pitch black though; Dara's sparks snuffed out in the movement.

We take a moment to catch our breath. Dara checks their palms, and as they light a new spark, I can see grazes on the skin. That must smart. Everyone seems okay, if a bit bruised, and so we keep going.

Luckily the path flattens out and the tunnel walls peel away. To be safe, Dara snuffs out their spark so all that remains is the gloomy, sparse light from the cave crystals. As our eyes adjust, I realise we're in another cavern. Chia curves the sound barrier around us, a thin layer of bubble wrap in the air.

In the distance, someone cries.

We glance at each other nervously, knowing it could be a trick. Or it could be one of the kids that were stolen. We won't know until we get there.

In my head, I repeat the mission to myself. Find Stevie. Find the other kids. Get everyone out of here, taking out as many coraniaids we can.

With only the light from the crystals to see by,

Dara guides us along the wall. We walk in a line, close enough to touch, but with our hands unlinked. Just in case we need them.

My head swims with the sound as is gets louder, and louder.

We pass a huge cluster of crystals just as a rattle cuts through the air. Gone is the crying, and right above us in the distance I see the dim glow of four red eyes.

In one fluid turn, Chia throws a bubble around the coraniaid. Miraculously, it doesn't notice as she makes it big enough to cover that whole section of the ceiling.

It can't hear us.

But it could still see us if we're not careful.

I point at the net-gun and Dara shakes their head. It's way too high up to reach, and if we missed, we'd be sending up a firework which would give us away.

Before we move on, I look around the cavern for the tell-tale red blink of any other eyes, but I can't see any others. Neither can Dara from the shake of their head. Chia's eyes are turned upwards as she concentrates on keeping the sound bubble up and unnoticeable.

I guide her forward, as we continue along the edge of the cavern, Dara pausing to help her around debris in her path. There are less crystals here, and the darkness grows around us.

This is taking so long that I worry Stevie's going to think we didn't make it in after her.

Ahead, Dara slows, raising a hand so that we stop. Together, we work to guide Chia – who is still concentrating on the coraniaid above us – around a pile of something.

It's only as I step after her that my foot lands on something loose. There's a loud scratch as my foot slides under me, and Dara gasps.

For a blissful moment, nothing happens.

That is, until a rattle sounds through the cavern, and we all realise that we're not alone.

There's another coraniaid in here with us.

I see it rushing straight towards us, the stamp of its feet against the rock echoing around the cave.

I leap in front of Chia and Dara, drawing Excalibur in a sweeping arc.

The blade meets flesh, and the beast recoils away from us with a hiss.

In the lowlight, I can see it is smaller than the others I've fought. I advance with my blade forward, pushing it back away from Chia. She must concentrate on the coraniaid above us, and if Dara uses their powers, that one will see the flashing.

This is all on me. All we can hope is that it's dark enough down here that it can't see me and this other coraniaid fighting.

Stevie trained me well, even if it was just for a day. I can do this.

"Come on then," I whisper, knowing it can hear me. Its beady red eyes lock onto mine.

It rushes me again, so I do the same. I barrel into its chest with my shoulder and hack with Excalibur. The monster shrieks and turns, and I swipe again. These moves wouldn't be allowed on a fencing piste, but fighting dirty is all I have. And I feel, almost, in control. I'm not desperately hacking away. Now, I know where to point this sword, how to move, how to stand. I've taken what she taught me and combined it with my instincts, into something entirely new. A fighting style that's all me.

The coraniaid staggers, one leg propped against a wall. We must have moved across the whole cavern in our fight. I want to look back for Chia and Dara, but I have to concentrate. And in the glow of a crystal, I can see a deep gash in the coraniaid's chest. It's weak.

With a flick of the lid, I throw a sphere of water straight into its face. It shakes, disorientated, and that's when I squeeze. In response, the water forms a rope that wraps around its body. Just like the ones the afanc used on me.

It scrabbles, desperately trying to get free.

But with one hand on the rope, and Excalibur in the other, I thrust the blade deep into its chest.

The coraniaid crumples, like a long-dead spider. There's no flame, no smoke. It just flops over. For a moment, I think perhaps it's playing dead, until slowly it fades into nothing.

I breath deep. Killing doesn't bring me any joy, but it does feel like I'm settling a score, at least. One less monster in the world. Or worlds, I suppose.

Some of the water returns to my bottle when I call it, bringing with it luminous specks of coraniaid blood. In the crystal light, I can see the bottle is about three quarters full. I still need to work on recalling water.

I sprint back to Dara and Chia who look slightly horrified by my performance.

"Wow," whispers Dara, the net gun in their hands. "I had this ready but . . . wow."

"Let's go quickly," I say. The first coraniaid still hasn't noticed us, or the streaks of lime green blood splattered everywhere, but I don't want to push our luck.

We keep going and luckily we're back in a tunnel after a few more steps. The second one must've been walking past us at the exact right time.

The crying has disappeared, I realise. I don't know if that's a good or a bad sign, or if it was even any of the others. In the Unlands, nothing is as it seems.

Up ahead I can see the tunnel split again, and to my surprise and relief, I find some markings on the wall. They're not mine and Stevie's infinity sign – it's Chia's moon, with an arrow pointing towards one of the tunnels.

Just as I'm about to ask if that means the way she went or where she'd been, a sound cuts through the air.

It's a familiar angry shriek, echoing from the other tunnel. The one Chia's symbol didn't point to.

"Get off me!"

It's Stevie.

Before I can stop them, Dara runs down the tunnel.

"No, Dara!" hisses Chia. "Stop! Don't go that way!"

That's when I know it's a trap.

But Dara is running straight into it, and we can't leave them.

"Come on," I say, and Chia and I race after them.

The thing is, knowing you've made a horrible mistake doesn't make the reality of it any less terrible.

Right up ahead, in a dead-end cavern brightly lit by a shimmering portal on the other side, is the biggest coraniaid I've ever seen. Its huge legs are strong and broad, and its body is thick with muscle. The eyes are wild, all-seeing and stare right at us. I'm not sure I've ever seen a coraniaid's mouth before – I've been too busy avoiding their grabbing, sweeping, punching legs. But this one has a wide mouth full of teeth, pulled open in a horrible grin.

I get the sense that it's pleased to see us.

And that's when it does the creepiest thing in the world.

"Get off me! Get off me! Get off me!" it cries in Stevie's voice.

Chapter Thirty

Dara is all fury. Sparks stand their hair on end and swarm over their skin, the purple so dark it moves between red and black. There's no stopping them as they race straight to the coraniaid.

I reach for the water at my side, but with horror feel something wet running down my leg. I didn't shut the lid after the last fight, and so the bottle is almost empty. Behind me are a trail of soggy footsteps. When I pull at them, a few drops return to the bottle, but that's it.

Come on, I urge, as Dara dances around the coraniaid.

But no more comes. I'm almost out of water.

The monster easily dodges Dara's attacks. Its movements are so swift and effortless, despite its enormous size. There's something different about this one. And I'm pretty sure it knows it is way stronger than us.

With the flick of one long insectoid leg, it flings Dara through the air.

They collide into me. We land hard and tangled in each other, and all the air is knocked out of me. I can't breathe.

It turns to reach for us, but it's battered back against the chamber wall by a rushing gust of air.

"Come on. We've got to get out of here," Chia urges as she pulls us to our feet. I wince in pain and look down to see blood. When Dara landed on me, I landed on Excalibur. A cut runs down my leg.

"No," Dara snaps. "It must have her. How else would it have her voice?"

Before we can argue, Dara shoots sparking darts at the coraniaid. It escapes Chia's grasp and dodges every single one.

I raise my sword, but the cut in my leg makes me wince,

"Where is she!?" Dara yells at it, panting with effort as a large ball of electricity builds between their hands. Their hair stands on end. And everything, including us, is lit purple.

A rattle sounds behind us, and I realise with horror that in using her power to save us, Chia let go of the vacuum around the coraniaid.

And she didn't throw one up when we ran in here, so . . . we can be heard throughout the Unlands.

Another coraniaid lurches behind us, probably the one from the cavern we just left. I regret not taking it out while we were in there.

And now there's two and we are trapped between them. I'm out of water,

We're dead if we don't come up with a new plan.

The net gun is slung on Dara's side, and I see them reach for it, but with all the weaving and dodging, they don't have time to stop and use it.

"Hold this one back, Chia," I yell. She nods, and I race towards Dara and the huge coraniaid with Excalibur drawn.

I rush forward, just like last time. But this fight is not going to be anywhere near as easy.

I swing hard, but the monster parries my attack with a leg. The air rings with metal. I leap back, and its riposting glances past my chest. The pain from my leg howls through me and I slip on the uneven ground. Sensing my weakness, a second leg slams into my body. I skid hard across the ground, and Excalibur flies off across the cavern. My skin is on fire, and my vision blurs. I retch.

"No, come get *me*, you massive brute!" screams Dara, and the huge coraniaid turns back to them.

The rattling grows louder, and I hear Chia cry out with the effort of holding the other one back.

"Chia!" I screech, as I see her blurry figure fall to the floor, exhausted.

The coraniaid in the tunnel screams with delight, and rears up, ready to strike. I scrabble to right myself, but I'm so dizzy, and my sword is out of reach. I'm unarmed, and half-knocked out, and Chia is about to—

There's a huge metallic clonk, and suddenly the monster falls back, away from Chia.

Gelert appears from the tunnel and leaps on top of the fallen coraniaid. Teeth meet flesh and he growls with fury. It's weird seeing Gelert fight, but he's ferocious. With one great tear, bright green blood splatters everywhere.

My eyesight clears as he hops down from the coraniaid which seems to melt into the floor. He's joined by Stevie and her baseball bat, both covered in green blood.

Stevie. It's actually her. She's safe, if a bit blood splattered.

Gelert helps Chia to her feet, but she's exhausted and leans hard against him.

Just as I whip round to tell Dara, they scream.

The huge beast backs them into a corner.

I'm unarmed but I have to do something.

That's when I realise that I'm right by the glittering portal. On the other side is a world that is definitely not our own; or at least it's definitely not Britain. Lush plants I've never seen before, a waterfall in the distance, and strange creatures flying in the sky. It reminds me of a rainforest, but lit gold like a filtered photo.

Wait. Waterfall.

Water.

Before I can think about whether it's a good idea, I thrust my hand through, and scream.

The portal scorches my skin like fire. It warps and burns, bubbles rising, but I can't stop even though everything in my body is telling me to.

It hurts. It hurts like nothing else I've ever felt

before, and I'm so, so angry. Angry that I'm fighting. Angry that we moved. Angry that we have to stop Arawn and rescue the kids, even though we're only kids ourselves. I just want to live a normal life.

The anger rushes through me, hot and red and leaping.

And if in answer, the water sails towards me.

"Dara, MOVE" I scream.

I whip my arm back through portal, dragging a waterfall with me.

Dara leaps out of the way just as the water smashes into the coraniaid.

The monster slams into the wall and before it can move, I pull all the water, a whole waterfall's worth, around the coraniaid in a bubble prison.

And with the last of my energy, I crush.

There's a series of sickening noises as the coraniaid's body gives way under the weight of the water.

I don't let go until I'm sure it's dead.

Its body falls warped under the weight of the water, under the weight of my power, but still I don't let go. The hot anger courses through me still, and I need to know that it's dead. That it can't hurt us.

I feel a nudge at my elbow, a gentle calming touch.

342

"It's okay Vivi. You can let go," whispers Gelert. "We're safe."

So, I do.

I fall to my knees. And this time, I really do vomit.

But Gelert's right, it's gone. Dead. Like the others, its body disappears into the aether.

All that remains is one metallic leg that must have torn off when I threw it, which Stevie pokes with her baseball bat. "Ew," she says, and slightly loopy with relief, we all burst into exhausted laughter.

"Stevie, I—" says Dara, limping towards her, but before they can say anything else, she pulls them into a hug. After a moment they leap apart, cheeks pink with embarrassment.

To my horror, Stevie picks up the leg and slings it around her shoulders like the world's most horrible shawl.

"You're keeping that?" I moan.

"I thought Dara might want it," Stevie sniffs, and they beam at her.

"Look at you scavenging for me. You're so nice."

"Don't get used to it.

Gelert helps me to my feet. I feel terrible and probably look it. But Chia looks ashen. This was her

343

first fight with us all, after all. And she did so much. She steadies an arm on Gelert's back, and I am so thankful that he's an Irish Wolfhound and big enough to support both of us.

Stevie hands me Excalibur, rescued from across the cavern, and I slide it back into its scabbard, glad to have the weight of it at my hip again.

"Are there more?" I croak.

"We took out the one that was guarding me and the other kids," Stevie says.

"I can't smell any others," adds Gelert. "Just a lot of unwashed children."

As if on cue, the stolen kids pour down the tunnel clinging to each other.

"You found them," cries Chia with relief.

I recognise a few of their faces from the forum – Clare Woodfine and Jason Ortega – but there are about seven of them all together. Grubby and hunger-starved and scared.

"Let's not stick around to find out if the whole Unlands heard us," I say, relieved that we're all together.

We found Stevie. We killed the coraniaids. Now we just have to get everyone out of here.

"Wait, where is Isabella?" bleats Chia.

"This is everyone we found," says Stevie.

"Isabella. Red hair, white skin, lots of freckles. She was here when I was?" she asks the survivors, and while they seem to know who she means, no one knows where she is.

Everyone looks so drained.

"Isabella?" calls Chia again.

"Maybe she got out already?" offers Dara.

And that's when I feel prickles at the back of my neck. Like I'm being watched.

Slowly, I turn back to the portal with the waterfall.

Ice runs down my spine as I catch a pair of eyes in the distance. Dark, furious eyes.

They belong to a girl.

A girl with red hair, and freckles.

And a look of betrayal clearly written on her face.

"Oh no," I moan.

We missed someone.

Everyone spins around to the portal.

"Isabella!" cries Chia. "We have to help her!"

Goosebumps rise on my skin as I see a great hand rest on Isabella's shoulder.

"Oh my god," mutters Stevie.

And then, Isabella disappears.

"We need to get out of here. Now," commands Gelert.

"No! We can't! We didn't save everyone," I protest, my voice joined in a weak, desperate chorus with Chia's.

I drag myself to the portal, and thrust my hand through, but the burning pain is too much. I shriek, recoiling. There's nothing we can do. I can't follow her, not without burning myself up. But I can't leave her. We can't leave her.

I fight and struggle, and it's all a blur, but Gelert bites onto the back of my clothes and I'm too weak to pull free.

As Gelert drags me away, I blink in and out of consciousness.

Everything goes dark.

Chapter Thirty-One

"Nimuë?"

My voice echoes over the water.

For a moment, I'm afraid she won't come. Like somehow, I broke the sword and our connection in that horrible fight, but she appears out of the mist, walking on the water as if it were land.

She throws her arms around me.

"You're okay," she whispers.

As she lets go, I catch sight of myself in the water. There are no bruises, no dark lines under my eyes.

No scarring from the portal.

"Trust me, I don't look this good in person."

Her eyes cloud over with concern.

"I'm okay, don't worry. I just look like I've been through it," I say with a laugh.

The burn on my arm is raw and hurts like heck, but I was managing to hide it from the Mums with a combo of long sleeves and gloves, though they are agony to take on and off.

As if she knows or can see the truth, Nimuë takes my arm in her hand and strokes it. I flinch, expecting it to hurt, but it doesn't, even if her fingers are deathly cold.

"Is Gelert still with you?"

"Yes, he's at home with me."

On the way out of the coraniaid nest, I had asked him to come live with me and the Mums instead of disappearing off into the Unlands, or, as I suspected, back to Beddgelert. He had sighed deeply and said, "It was a kind of home once. It's hard to forget that, even after all these years."

Weirdly, the Mums found my sudden new enormous dog the least surprising part of everything. Mam said she'd been thinking about getting me a dog, though admittedly not one quite so large, and I figured we had at least a decade before I had to broach the immortal ghost part of the conversation with them. Apparently finding him in a park was a good enough description, and unsurprisingly he didn't have a microchip. And so, he became ours. Well, as much as he'd let himself be.

He relented on the no-collars-issue quickly, especially as Mumma chose him an expensive looking tweed one. I'm not sure he'll ever be comfortable on a lead though.

"Did you manage to rescue everyone?" Her voice is so hopeful that my heart breaks.

"No. We . . . we missed someone."

Nimuë doesn't say anything, knowing that platitudes are not going to make this better. Yes, we did save a bunch of people. But we still missed someone. She's still trapped there. With Arawn.

When we'd gotten back to the park with the stolen kids, we had called the police with an anonymous tip, voiced by Gelert. The weirdest thing was that when they arrived with some of the parents, none of the parents thought their kids had been missing at all. Even though there were alerts in the system, and we all looked like we'd been through a war. None of the adults could explain it, but the police decided it must have been an error and we all got a lecture about wasting police time.

Naturally, everyone on *Strange Britain* has been

speculating about it. The Ghost Queen has sent me an email to say she was glad we were back safe.

"You have to take each victory, even if it's not a perfect one," she says slowly, and I know she's not just trying to make me feel better about it. "This is just the beginning, Vivi. You still have your greatest fights ahead of you. You still have to find the rest of the calonnau. And then stop Arawn."

At his name, the eyes spring to mind. The hand on Isabella's shoulder. The glittering world beyond.

"What's Annwn like?"

Her face glows softly. "So beautiful. Lush and rich with wonders."

"And gold? Everything looks golden, right?"

She pauses. "Why . . . yes. Vivi how did you know that?"

"I think I've seen it, finally. There was a portal we found in the Unlands. We were fighting a corani-aid and I could see a waterfall through the portal, so I stuck my hand through and took the water." She licks her lips. "And that's where the last person was. On the other side."

"Of course. To serve him," she spits.

"What do you mean serve him?" I feel sick to

my stomach.

"Be commanded by him, meet his every need. He's very clever, so half the time they don't even think they've been charmed. What better weapon against your enemies than one of their own."

She stares hard into the water. "He tried to take my children once, or he threatened to, if I didn't help him. That's why I went to Rhiannon in the first place. I didn't want my babies to be his playthings. She knows what it's like to have a child taken by evil."

"He tried to blackmail you?"

"Among many other things," she says sadly.

"Oh come, come Nimmy. It wasn't all that bad was it?"

My whole body freezes as a new voice cuts through everything. Deep, rich, and a little too pleased with itself.

I turn, and see a very tall man, dressed in rich gold and blood-red. His hair is a thick dark gold, all the way through to his beard, and he's big, made of pure stocky muscle. A man who rides and hunts.

And his eyes . . . I recognise those dark eyes.

Nimuë springs back, shielding me with her body.

"Arawn," she hisses. "What are you doing here?"

"King Arawn, I'll remind you. I wanted to meet your little friend. Or, I suppose, the new you?"

He walks towards us, purpose in every step. Nimuë shrinks, but stands firm, protecting me with her whole body.

"How did you get in here? You should still be trapped in Annwn."

He chuckles, far too pleased with himself. "Oh it wasn't so hard. You aren't that clever, Nimmy. A soul connection isn't so hard to reach into, especially when you're using Otherworld space. I thought you'd be smarter than that, putting your sweet little calon at risk like this."

He laughs heartily.

I hate this guy.

"You're a monster," she snarls. "Get away from us."

He enjoys her fear, I can see it. "If you must be so insistent about it, I will leave you for now, my daughter."

"Your . . . dad? He's your dad?" I croak.

I can't see the resemblance, though they are both impossibly beautiful. Her beauty is pure, elegant; his seems cruel.

"He's no true *father* of mine," she growls. "Blood is

nothing to him. Why should it matter to me either?"

He turns his eyes on me, and I feel them boring into the core of me.

"We will meet again, young Vivi. And next time, I will not be quite so courteous. It's rather adorable that you think you can prevent me from getting what will be mine. Don't be fools; you will not stop me a second time."

"We will," I say, trying to be brave but my voice wavers and Arawn hears the hesitation. He laughs, a deep boom like a lion's roar, and suddenly I feel afraid. Terribly, terribly afraid.

In one swift movement, Arawn pushes Nimuë into the water before leaning down towards me, clutching my face in his huge hand. "You will learn where your true place lies, Vivian."

And with that, I wake up.

This isn't over yet.

It's just beginning.

GLOSSARY

PEOPLE

Arawn *(ar-ah-un)*: the King of the Annwn, one of the Kingdoms of Other.

Ceridwen *(keh-rid-when)*: a powerful witch of legend who lived on an island in Lake Bala. She is the creator of a magical cauldron.

Emrys *(em-ris)*: a mysterious boy in the Unlands.

Gelert *(geh-ler-t)*: formerly a dog owned by King Llywelyn, and now a ghost dog who helps the calonnau.

Llywelyn *(ll-ew-el-in*)*: An ancient King in Wales who loved to hunt.

Myrddin *(mur-thin)*: also known as Merlin, a wizard of myth who guided King Arthur.

Nimuë *(nim-way)*: the Lady of the Lake who gifted the sword Excalibur to King Arthur.

Pwyll *(puh-ll*)*: The Prince of Dyfed, a kingdom in Wales.

Rhiannon *(rhi-an-non)*: an Otherworld woman who falls in love with and marries Pwyll.

* in Welsh, a ll is a letter in our alphabet. It can be a little tricky to pronounce, but if you put your tongue tip at the roof of your mouth behind your teeth and then gently blow air around the sides of your tongue, you'll get a soft kind of hiss noise. This is all!

PLACES

Annwn *(ah-noon)*: a shimmering-gold Kingdom in the Other, ruled over by King Arawn. Sometimes mistaken for Avalon from Arthurian legend, or the afterlife – it is neither.

The Kingdoms of Other: Another world alongside our own, split into various Kingdoms including Annwn.

The Unlands: The gaps between the Otherworld and our world. It looks like a rabbit warren of crystal lit caves. Gelert sometimes travels the world using them.

OTHER WORDS

Awl (*all*): A metal tool with a sharp end, usually used for making holes, particular used for leather-working.

Calon (*cah-lon*): a person in a partnered soul connection with someone else e.g. Vivi is Nimuë's calon, and Nimuë is also Vivi's calon. The plural is calonnau *(cah-lon-eye)*.

Excalibur: An enchanted sword, made by the Lady of the Lake, Nimuë. She gifted it to King Arthur after his first sword was lost

Talisman: a key item linked to each calon pair. When a talisman is found, their powers wake up. These were scattered all over the UK by the spellcasters.

Hiraeth (*hear-eye-th*): a deep longing for something, usually home.

Acknowledgements

I've been trying to find a way to tell this story for a long, long time, and now, reader, it belongs to you. There are a lot of people I need to thank for their involvement over the years, in ways big and small, but without whom this book would not be a book.

To Abi, my agent: you were the first person I ever showed this book to, and it meant the world to me that you fell in love with it. Thank you for letting me borrow your name. I'm honoured to have you guide me and my career.

To Eishar: you saw what I was trying to do with this book, including what I was too nervous to try, and your guidance and trust in me made this story what it is. I literally could not have done this without you, and I'm so grateful to be able to work with you on a project of my heart.

Thank you too to Aimée for giving this book at home with Knights Of. Thank you to everyone in the wider Knights Of family for their hard work and love for this book including Sophie, Annabelle, Courtney, Ella, Sam, Emilie, Imogen, Dee and Elizabeth.

Thank you to Harry Woodgate for the beautiful cover and for the lovely DMs as you read the book. Many thanks to Caleb River for their read and kind comments.

Writing is a solitary job by nature, but I'm blessed to know some other excellent authors and book people. Thank you to Lee Newbery for kindly talking over some Welsh language thoughts with me. Thank you to Elle McNicoll for the encouragement and advice over the years. Thank you to my author and book world friends who have helped me along the way, especially Ash, Charlie, Darran, Melissa, LD, Lucy, Kiran, Tom, Melinda, Kat, Samantha, Aisha, Katie, Louie, Stephanie, Connie, Faridah, Susie, Ella, Ben, Robin, Lex. Thank you to the members of the debut groups for the cheering: debut 22 chat 2, 2023 kidlit chin-waggers and the aptly named 'can I call myself a real writer now?'

Many more friends than I can possibly name here have supported and loved me over the years while I wrote this book. Back when I was trying to work out what story I was trying to tell, Nell would listen to me fight through plot holes and too many ideas. Thank you for all the thoughtful advice. Special thanks to Jade and Amelia for helping me come up with early names for this series when it was about to go on submission, and I realised "magical squad" was actually not a title. Thank you to Murder Cat gang for celebrating Vivi with me in Portugal. My writing grows everyday thanks to cowriting with ElleHa – thank you for all the sprints. Thank you to Slice & Lauren for looking after me so much over the last year; I am so grateful to have such wonderful friend-family.

Many thanks to the Williams branch of the family for the love. Mary Ann and Derek listened to me work through early iterations of this book with kindness and enthusiasm while we lived with them, and for that space and time I'll be forever grateful. Thank you to Geoff, Steph, Léon, Poppy & Siméon for all the love.

Thank you to my parents Aliy and Keith for nurturing my reading and taking me adventuring to find stories writ on the land. Finally coming home in

May 2022 was just magical. This story exists because of you both, in many ways! Thank you to my sister Julie, my brother-in-law James for the encouragement and love, and nephews Dylan and Theo for being the most brutal Among Us players in the world.

This is now the third book in which I've apologised to Nerys for ignoring her while I write, but also Gelert came from her grumpy mannerisms so she should be glad she is somewhat immortalised in fiction, even if she can't read.

Finally, forever thanks to my partner Tim for taking me for stomps and scoots in the woods so I can work out plot issues. Our walks together during lockdown helped keep this book, and me, moving forward. All my words exist thanks to you.

AND HER FRIENDS
WILL RETURN IN 2024

Lizzie Huxley-Jones

Author

Lizzie Huxley-Jones (they/them) is an autistic author and editor based in London. They are the author of the queer holiday rom-com *Make You Mine This Christmas* (2022) from Hodder Studio and fantasy middle grade series *Vivi Conway and the Sword of Legend* (2023) from Knights Of. They write joyful stories that centre queerness and disability.

They are the editor of *Stim*, an anthology of autistic authors and artists, which was published by Unbound in April 2020 to coincide with World Autism Awareness Week. They are also the author of the children's biography *Sir David Attenborough: A Life Story* (2020) and a contributor to the anthology *Allies: Real Talk About Showing Up, Screwing Up, And Trying Again* (2021), which was chosen to be a World Book Day Title for 2023, renamed as *Being an Ally* (2023). They tweet too much at @littlehux, taking breaks to walk their dog Nerys.

Harry Woodgate
Illustrator

Harry Woodgate (pronouns: they/them) is an award-winning author and illustrator who has worked with clients including National Book Tokens, Google, The Sunday Times Magazine, Harper Collins, Simon & Schuster, Walker Books, Knights Of, Andersen Press, Bloomsbury, The Washington Post and Penguin Random House.

Their debut author-illustrator title, *Grandad's Camper*, won the Waterstones Children's Book Prize Best Illustrated Book 2022 and a Stonewall Book Award Honor from the American Library Association, as well as being shortlisted for the inaugural Polari Children's & YA Prize 2022 and nominated for the CILIP Yoto Kate Greenaway Award. Their other books include *Grandad's Pride*, *Timid*, *Little Glow*, *Shine Like The Stars*, *My First Baking Book* and *The Very Merry Murder Club*.

Harry is passionate about writing and illustrating diverse, inclusive stories that inspire children to be inquisitive, creative, kind and proud of what makes them unique. When they're not making books, they love writing music, cycling, baking, and exploring independent coffee shops, gardens and bookstores.

KNIGHTS OF

KNIGHTS OF is a multi award-winning inclusive publisher focused on bringing underrepresented voices to the forefront of commercial children's publishing. With a team led by women of colour, and an unwavering focus on their intended readership for each book, Knights Of works to engage with gatekeepers across the industry, including booksellers, teachers and librarians, and supports non-traditional community spaces with events, outreach, marketing and partnerships.